TRAPPED IN TERROR

The elevator shuddered to a halt. Nancy grabbed the handle, eager to get out, but nothing happened. Frank also yanked on the handle. It wouldn't budge.

"We're trapped in here and no one knows where we are!" Allison said.

Frank swept the beam of his flashlight around the top of the elevator. "It looks like there's a hinged door in the ceiling."

"One of us can climb onto the roof of the elevator," Nancy said. "Then jump into the hall and try to open the door from the other side." All at once Nancy smelled smoke. Looking down, she noticed a gray cloud curling up from under the door.

"A fire!" Allison squealed.

Nancy's heart raced as the smoke swirled around her ankles, covering the floor like ground fog. Whirling, she faced Frank and Allison. "If we don't get out of here, we'll suffocate!"

Nancy Drew & Hardy Boys SuperMysteries

Double Crossing
A Crime for Christmas
Shock Waves
Dangerous Games
The Last Resort
The Paris Connection
Buried in Time
Mystery Train
Best of Enemies
High Survival
New Year's Evil
Tour of Danger
Spies and Lies
Tropic of Fear
Courting Disaster
Hits and Misses
Evil in Amsterdam
Desperate Measures

Passport to Danger
Hollywood Horror
Copper Canyon Conspiracy
Danger Down Under
Dead on Arrival
Target for Terror
Secrets of the Nile
A Question of Guilt
Island of Intrigue
Murder on the Fourth of July
High Stakes
Nightmare in New Orleans
Out of Control
Exhibition of Evil
At All Costs
Royal Revenge
Operation: *Titanic*
Process of Elimination

Available from ARCHWAY Paperbacks

A NANCY AND HARDY DREW AND BOYS SUPER MYSTERY™

AT ALL COSTS

Carolyn Keene

AN ARCHWAY PAPERBACK
Published by POCKET BOOKS
New York London Toronto Sydney Tokyo Singapore

AN ARCHWAY PAPERBACK *Original*

An Archway Paperback published by
POCKET BOOKS, a division of Simon & Schuster Inc.
1230 Avenue of the Americas, New York, NY 10020

ISBN: 0-671-00734-3

First Archway Paperback printing October 1997

10 9 8 7 6 5 4 3 2

Cover art by Franco Accornero

Printed in the U.S.A.

IL 6+

AT ALL COSTS

Chapter

One

TAKE A LOOK at that view," Frank Hardy said, his gaze sweeping over the snow-capped mountain peaks that jutted up into an intense blue sky.

"The Wasatch Mountains are awesome," his brother, Joe, agreed. "I can't wait to ski them."

The Hardys were walking through the glass-enclosed terminal of the Salt Lake City International Airport with their friend, Kip Coles. Kip worked as a wilderness adventure guide, and when he'd heard the Hardys were going to be in Utah over Thanksgiving vacation, he'd arranged for the three to do some extreme skiing in northern Utah's pristine backcountry.

"You won't believe how great the powder is," Kip said as he led them to the baggage-claims area. He was a tall, lanky twenty-year-old with curly brown hair and a perpetual tan from being outside year-round. "Snow has been dumped in the mountains since mid-October. The skiing will be super."

"Count me in!" Joe said, his blue eyes twinkling.

Eighteen-year-old Frank pushed back a strand of his dark hair as he grinned at his brother. "I knew you'd want to head for the slopes the instant we arrived. Too bad that our case has to come first."

"Hey, I can always find time for fun," Joe countered.

Frank halted in the crowded baggage area. The terminal was filled with holiday travelers, and right then he wished that he and Joe were there on vacation. He had to remind himself that they were in Utah to do a job, to hunt down some dangerous saboteurs.

"There's our stuff." Joe darted forward and grabbed their ski bags and suitcases off the revolving carousel, then he handed a couple to Frank.

After they'd retrieved everything, Kip led them to his Jeep, parked alongside the curb.

"Let's just hope this case isn't as dangerous as the one we tackled last time you were here," Kip said as he unlocked the doors. While hiking in the southeastern Utah desert, Kip and the Hardys had helped save two teens lost in the wilderness and captured a heavily armed escaped con.

"It could be," Frank said solemnly. He loaded the last of the luggage into the four-by-four, then climbed in back. "At least the state's Building and Games Committee was worried enough to contact my father for help."

Kip looked at Frank in the rearview mirror as he steered the vehicle away from the terminal. "The newspapers are still reporting the construction problems at the new Sports Park as 'accidents' and 'delays.'"

Joe snorted. "Perfectly executed accidents, you mean. Each time something goes wrong at one of the sites, it's been major enough to cause construction to shut down. Thankfully, the Building and Games Committee finally agreed the mishaps were too serious to ignore. Fortunately, no one's been hurt—yet."

"And they're suspecting saboteurs?" Kip asked.

"They're not sure." Leaning forward, Frank rested one arm on the back of Joe's seat. "But they want to find out what's going on before negative publicity jeopardizes Utah's opportunity to host the 2002 winter Olympics."

Kip whistled. "Now I see the problem. The state figures the Olympics will bring in hundreds of millions in revenue." He shook his head. "Not that everybody in Utah is eager to host the Olympics."

"Oh?" Frank raised one brow.

"Environmentalists are especially concerned," Kip explained. "Every year Salt Lake City holds the Utah Winter Games, but hosting the Olympics is a huge deal. It means more construction and millions of visitors. There are lots of us who'd like Utah to stay unpopulated and unspoiled."

Joe glanced over his shoulder at Frank. Frank could tell his brother was wondering the same thing. Could environmentalists be sabotaging the new Sports Park? It was worth looking into, since bad press or the possibility that the facilities might not be ready could force the International Olympic Committee to award the games to some other state.

Frank glanced out the window at the mountains that rose dramatically behind the Salt Lake City skyline. Northern Utah was gorgeous, and he could see why many people didn't want it to change.

Turning off the highway, Kip headed into the mountains. The Hardys would be staying at the Coleses' condo in Park City, a resort town and skiers' paradise.

"Well, count me in on helping discover what's going on," Kip said. "Like I told you on the phone, my uncle Walt owns the construction company building the facilities for the bobsled."

"Crew contacts would be great," Frank said.

"We're working undercover as security guards on the Building and Games Security Committee, but we can use all the help we can get. So far we don't have any leads."

"And we need to find out what's going on," Joe said, his voice grim. "Before somebody gets hurt during one of these so-called accidents!"

"Nice digs, Allison," Nancy Drew said. She dropped her duffel bag on the floor of her friend's dorm suite and looked around the tiny bedroom. It opened into a central living area, which was simply furnished with a wood-frame couch, a couple of chairs, and several patterned rugs.

"Really! This is my idea of dorm life," George Fayne said as she plopped down her suitcase on Allison's bed.

"I couldn't agree more," Allison Fernley replied. Nineteen-year-old Allison was a year older than her two friends from River Heights. Her interest in environmental studies had brought her to Utah, where she was a sophomore at the university. "Still, I do have to share this space with three other girls. And believe me, it gets crowded, especially when we're all trying to get ready for something at the same time."

George grinned and sat on the edge of the bed. "Doesn't sound too bad to me. Though I'm glad your other roommates are home for Thanksgiving. I can't see six of us living here."

"Me, either." Hands on hips, Nancy went over to a large picture window. Salt Lake City was spread out in the valley below her. "I'm sure glad you invited us out for some Thanksgiving skiing."

Allison picked up Nancy's bag and set it on the bed next to George's. "Hey, it's all my pleasure. It's great to see faces from River Heights. Sometimes I get homesick."

"Homesick!" George exclaimed. "With great classes, beautiful scenery, oodles of winter sports, and a new boyfriend? How can you possibly be homesick?"

Allison laughed. "Well, believe it or not, you don't notice the scenery after a while. And I'm not a sports nut like you, George. But you're right, the classes are great."

"And how about Tyler?" Nancy teased. Every letter Allison had written to her for the past month had been filled with news about Tyler Conklin, a student Allison had met at an environmental rally.

A rosy blush spread over Allison's cheeks. "Okay. He's great, too. I can't wait for you to meet him tonight at dinner."

George clamped a hand over her stomach. "Oooo, talking about dinner, I'm starved. All we had was soda and peanuts on the plane."

Nancy walked over to Allison and put an arm around her friend's shoulder. "Can we head over to the restaurant? After all, Tyler needs to hear high-school horror tales from a couple of old friends. Like about the time you got locked in the girls' bathroom."

"Or the time we were playing donkey basketball and you got bucked off," George added.

Allison's mouth fell open. "You wouldn't!"

Nancy laughed. "No. But we will tell him how lucky he is to be dating you. That *is* why you invited us to Utah, right?"

"I can't imagine where Tyler is," Allison said an hour later. For what seemed to be the hundredth time, she checked her watch and then looked over at the door of the restaurant.

"Something probably came up," Nancy said, reassuring her friend. She glanced down at Allison's untouched hamburger and fries. "So eat up. The food's great."

George nodded in agreement. "My chicken salad was perfect." She speared one of Nancy's pickles. "How was your turkey club, Nan?"

"Great." Nancy tried to sound cheerful as Allison grew increasingly gloomy.

Nancy thought wistfully about her own boyfriend, Ned Nickerson, who'd decided to go to Florida with friends for Thanksgiving. She wished she could be with him, but then reminded herself how much she'd been looking forward to skiing in Utah.

7

After tucking her reddish blond hair behind her ears, Nancy drank the last of her juice.

Again, Allison twisted around to look at the door, her brown eyes troubled.

"Do you think there's something wrong?" Nancy asked gently.

With a sigh, Allison turned back to her two friends. "I hope not. It's just that when I met Tyler he was in a relationship with another girl, and . . ." Her voice trailed off.

"And?" George prompted.

"And ever since he broke it off, the girl, Robyn, has been hounding him. They were pretty active in a radical environmental group called Earth at all Costs."

"I've heard of Earth at all Costs," George said. "I picked up one of their brochures at a rally in River Heights. They're into stuff like spiking trees to stop clear-cutting."

"Right. The group is a global network of environmental activists who feel they should use any means necessary, even violent ones, to stop big businesses that are threatening the earth. When I first met Tyler, he was pretty involved with them." Allison stared down at her clenched hands. "Then he changed. I like to think I helped him realize that the earth could be better protected by working through legal and peaceful means."

"So, Robyn wasn't only mad because Tyler

broke up with her, but also because he switched sides?" Nancy guessed.

Allison nodded glumly. "Now Tyler and I are active in a group on campus called Peace on Earth. Whenever I see Robyn she makes it clear how much she hates me."

"Does Tyler live on campus?" Nancy asked.

Allison shook her head, her tawny hair swinging against her cheeks. "No, he's in an apartment off campus."

Nancy waved to the waitress, signaling for their check. "Let's drive over and see if he's home."

Allison brightened. "Good idea."

Fifteen minutes later the three girls were driving through a neighborhood of Victorian houses and small apartment complexes.

"Cute houses," George said as she and Nancy peered out the windows.

"The area's called The Avenues," Allison said. "A lot of the old homes were made into apartments like the one Tyler's—" She stopped speaking and gasped. "There's a police car in front of Tyler's apartment!"

Jerking the car to the right, Allison parked in front of an older brownstone building and jumped out. Two white squad cars stood in the drive, their emergency lights flashing.

With a cry of distress, Allison raced up the walkway and into the building.

"What's going on?" George asked Nancy as they climbed out of the car.

"I have no idea, but let's find out," Nancy said as she jogged toward the brownstone.

The foyer was dark, but the girls could hear noise coming from the top of the stairs.

Taking the steps two at a time, Nancy and George reached the top floor, where they found a door partly open. Nancy could hear Allison's shrill voice coming from the other side. What was going on?

Nancy pushed inside, George right behind her. Allison was standing in the middle of a small efficiency apartment. She was flanked by two men, one in a police officer's uniform, the other in a suit. "Why are you here?" she was demanding. "Where's my boyfriend?"

"Excuse me, but may we have some ID?" the uniformed officer asked Allison. Reluctantly, she pulled her wallet from her purse.

Nancy stepped right up. "What's the matter?" She directed her question to the taller man in the suit. A police ID clipped to his suit lapel identified him as Detective Urich.

Movement from a small bedroom caught Nancy's attention. A man and a woman were moving slowly around the room, obviously searching the place. "Has something happened to Tyler?" she asked.

"No, ma'am," the detective answered. After checking Nancy and George's driver's licenses, he added, "But we sure would like to know where he is. Maybe you ladies can tell us."

"Not until you tell *us* what's going on," Nancy said firmly.

The detective pulled a matchstick from behind his ear and stuck it in his mouth. "Well . . ." He chewed on the stick for a moment, then said, "Seems your friend Tyler Conklin sent a letter to the American Progress corporate offices."

"So?" Allison propped her hands on her hips. "There's no law against that."

Nancy knew Allison was trying to be brave, though she could hear the quiver in her friend's voice.

"Except in the letter, he threatened to blow up the new ski-jump tower at the Sports Park if the company didn't meet his demands."

"What!" Nancy exclaimed. She glanced over at Allison. All the color had drained from her friend's face. Beside her, George was staring open-mouthed at the detective.

"That's crazy," Allison declared. "Tyler would never threaten anything like that."

The detective cocked his head. "Well, the evidence points to the fact that he *did* write the letter."

Nancy's gaze darted to the two officers in the bedroom. One was examining a computer. Had it been used to type the letter? Or was Detective Urich bluffing?

11

Taking the matchstick from his mouth, the detective pointed it at Allison. "And now your boyfriend seems to have disappeared, Miss Fernley. And he *is* a member of that crazy ecoterrorist group Earth at All Costs. That makes him look mighty guilty now, doesn't it."

Chapter

Two

"TYLER'S NO LONGER a member of Earth at All Costs," Allison protested.

"That's not what the membership roster says." Detective Urich pulled out a pad from his suit jacket. "Now, why don't you give me a list of places we might look for your boyfriend."

Allison bristled. "No way!"

"Allison"—Nancy put her hand on her friend's arm—"if you're sure Tyler couldn't have sent the letter, then you need to help the detective."

"Listen to Nancy," George urged. "She's worked with the police a lot."

Allison crossed her arms. "No," she repeated. "Detective Urich has already decided that Tyler is guilty. Let's go." Turning, she abruptly left the apartment. Nancy had no choice but to follow, though she was dying to see the letter Tyler had supposedly sent to American Progress.

"Allison!" Nancy caught up with her friend on the front lawn. "What is going on?"

Allison spun around to face Nancy and George. "Isn't it obvious? The police are accusing Tyler of something he didn't do."

George ran her fingers through her short dark hair. "None of this makes sense to me. What is American Progress, and what do they have to do with a ski jump?"

"It doesn't matter what American Progress is!" Allison said hotly. "Tyler is innocent—he wouldn't have written that letter. We have to warn him that the police are after him." Spinning away from her friends, Allison raced to her car.

Nancy and George exchanged glances.

"Boy, she's really upset," George said.

Nancy nodded. "And she should be if the police have faked evidence against Tyler. But if Allison wants us to help him, she's going to have to give us some explanations—fast."

"Here's the plan," Joe said to Frank and Kip the next morning. The three guys were in Kip's Jeep heading down Parley's Canyon from Park City. It was a gorgeous wintry day, the sun reflecting so brightly off the snow that Joe had donned his sunglasses. "We're meeting Roger Weems, the supervisor of the Building and Games Security Committee, at the new bobsled run of the Sports Park."

"Lucky for you two that my uncle Walt's company has almost finished the bobsled run." Kip took his eyes off the road for a second to grin at Joe, who was riding in the back. "And he just happens to need somebody to test it out. You game, Joe?"

"That sounds awesome! Count me in."

"Hey you two, aren't we supposed to be on a case?" Frank reminded them.

"Sure." Joe leaned forward, laughing. "As we whiz down the run, Kip and I can look for signs of sabotage."

Kip's grin turned to a frown. "Hey, don't even mention sabotage. My uncle's company is the only one that hasn't been plagued with problems."

"That's interesting." Joe rubbed his chin, trying to look serious. He couldn't stop thinking about the upcoming run on a bobsled, a sport he'd only watched on TV. "How many companies are involved in building the different venues?"

Kip shook his head as he steered down the winding mountain road. "You'll have to ask my uncle. Companies from all over Utah placed bids on the different construction jobs. The state is pouring millions into getting the Sports Park ready for this year's Winter Games. They should prove that Utah can host the Olympics."

"So any company that won a bid could make big money later for the Olympics." Frank twisted in his seat to look at Joe. "And there have to be plenty of disgruntled companies that didn't win bids."

"Right," Joe said. "Which gives us two leads to check out: the environmentalists, who may not want the construction in the first place, and those contractors who didn't win bids and get a piece of the pie."

Kip pointed out the window on the passenger side. "There's the Sports Park now. They're building part of it right into the mountainside."

Joe leaned down to get a better view. They were driving toward a huge area at the foot of a mountain that was cordoned off with chain-link fence.

Kip stopped at a security booth. The guard recognized Kip and waved him through.

"The guy didn't even check us out," Joe noted.

"I've been helping my uncle whenever I can," Kip explained. "The guard probably figured since you were with me, you must be okay."

Frank frowned. "Still, you'd think the Security Committee would have tightened security after the recent sabotage attempts."

"I agree," Joe said. "Let's suggest to Roger Weems that security check *everybody* entering the construction area."

Kip steered around an open area filled with cars, trucks, and construction equipment to park in front of a trailer. The sun had melted the snow in the lot and everything was muddy and wet.

In front of the trailer, a beefy man with a red face and a tall, slim girl were studying a blueprint. The girl wore earmuffs and a coverall and had the same brown curly hair as Kip.

"That's Shana, my cousin, and her father, my uncle Walt." Kip swung his door open, calling a cheery hello.

Joe climbed out from the back. Stretching, he glanced around the area, noting at least five more construction trailers nearby. "The state must have hired a lot of contractors," he said to Frank, who was looking around, his hand shading his eyes against the brilliant sunlight. Still, the November air was cold, and both brothers wore flannel shirts and goosedown vests.

"They did," Frank agreed. "The Sports Park is a huge project. They're either building or upgrading five venues: an ice-skating arena, speed-skating oval, ski-jump tower, downhill course, and the combined bobsled and luge track."

Joe frowned. "So there are hundreds of people who have legal access to the area. Any one of them could be a nut who's crazy enough to cause the accidents."

"Frank, Joe." Kip's uncle Walt approached them with a friendly smile and an outstretched hand. Joe shook it, wincing at the older man's firm grip. "Welcome to Utah. Kip tells me you're hanging around with the security crew?"

"Yes, sir," Frank said as he shook the older man's hand.

Uncle Walt whacked Frank on the shoulder. "Well, don't let Roger Weems get to you. He's a real stickler for details." He gestured for Kip's cousin to join them. "Let me introduce you to my daughter, Shana, the future owner of Coles Construction."

"Dad," Shana protested with a roll of her eyes. Ice-blue eyes, Joe noted, and creamy white skin. And even though her figure was hidden under her bulky coveralls, Joe could tell she was slim and long-legged like Kip.

"I'm not quite ready to take over," she explained, smiling at Frank and Joe. "Nor is Dad ready to retire," she kidded her father.

He chuckled. "True. But winters in Florida sound better and better all the time."

"You ready for us to test the bobsled run?" Kip asked. He was shifting anxiously from foot to foot, eager to go. "Joe's agreed to be brakeman."

Shana raised one brow and eyed Joe. Her gaze was so direct, Joe almost reddened. "You're going down the run with Krazy Kip?"

"Hey, we survived the desert together," Joe said.

"Oh, you're *that* Joe." She grinned at him.

"Kip told me a few stories about you. Still, do you think you're ready for *that?*" Turning, she pointed toward a mile-long iced track that started above them and snaked past them down the mountainside.

Joe gulped. "Sure," he replied quickly.

"Don't worry, we won't reach Olympic speeds," Kip assured him. "Maybe fifty miles an hour, tops."

"Fifty miles an hour?" This time Joe's voice cracked.

Shana, Frank, and Kip laughed.

"I've got Lycra suits, helmets, goggles, and racing shoes in the Jeep," Kip said. "We can change, then test that baby out. I can't wait."

"Me, either," Joe muttered when Kip had run back to the Jeep.

"While you two are having fun, I'm going to find Roger Weems," Frank told Joe. "We should report in."

Uncle Walt gestured toward a van in the parking lot. "He's here. That's his van. Though I'm surprised he's not in Provo, at Brigham Young University. That's where they're building the new speed-skating oval. Yesterday part of it collapsed unexpectedly. It's a huge mess."

"I'll see if I can find Weems," Frank said, wondering if the accident at the speed-skating oval was the latest sabotage attempt. He smacked his brother on the shoulder. "Don't fall off the sled," he called as he took off. Halfway to the trailer, he turned back, deciding to watch Joe's run down the mountain before seeing Weems.

Kip came up, his arms laden with gear. "We can change in the trailer."

Joe followed him inside. The trailer was filled with files, building materials, chairs, and two makeshift desks. Joe and Kip changed in a back room piled with boxes arranged like seats. Coffee cups, fast-food wrappers, and parts of the morning paper were strewn everywhere.

Joe zipped up the Lycra suit, which hugged his body like skin, then laced up the shoes, which had flexible spikes on the soles. While they dressed, Kip explained what Joe would have to do during the run. Joe noted that all the gear looked well-worn, and he hoped that meant Kip had lots of experience.

When the two stepped from the trailer, Shana eyed them appraisingly. "Not bad. You might almost pass for real Olympians," she joked.

Uncle Walt waved at the track. "We also need to recheck the best places to build the stations for the closed-circuit TV and camera crews," he told them. "So you may have to test the track several times."

Kip chuckled. "That shouldn't take long. Each descent takes only a minute or two."

"Fine with me," Joe said confidently as he followed Kip to the start house. But when he stood at the top of the run and looked down, he swallowed hard. There were fourteen curves and S-shaped twists built into the reinforced concrete track. At least they'd be barreling down it so fast he wouldn't have time to think about how scared he was.

"A good run depends on the initial start," Kip explained when they reached the sled. It was blue with white stripes and shaped like a small, round-nosed rocket. It also looked pretty beat-up, and Joe hoped it would make it down the run without falling apart.

The two put on their helmets. Grabbing the push-bar handles sticking up from the right side of the sled, Kip said, "Help me push it from the start house."

Joe went around to the left side. The sled had to be rocked, then shoved out of the push grooves in the track. Since a two-man sled weighed over eight hundred pounds, this was no easy task.

"In a race, there's an explosive beginning as the crew pushes the sled down the start track," Kip explained. "It passes through the starting gate and breaks an electric eye. We're going to take it a little slower.

"After corners one, two, and three, we'll hit the steepest part of the track," he continued. "As the driver, I'll be doing most of the work. If I take a curve too high, we could flip over. Too low and we could slam into the opposite wall. You only need to apply the brakes at the end."

Kip showed Joe how to work the brake at the back. "In a race, you'd be disqualified if you applied the brake during the run. But listen to me just in case we need it earlier. Ready?"

Joe slid his goggles over his eyes. "Ready."

The two got the sled moving faster, then Kip jumped into the front and grabbed the steering ropes. "Jump in!" he yelled over his shoulder.

Joe half-fell, half-leaped into the swiftly moving sled before helping Kip remove the push-bars. He barely had time to settle himself behind Kip when the sled picked up speed. Kip whooped loudly, and Joe grinned. It was great!

They hit the first set of curves, and the sled twisted sideways to the right, zoomed to the middle of the track, then twisted to the left. Joe felt his heart slam into his ribs. The icy wind whistled past, stinging his cheeks, but the speed was exhilarating.

Then a loud boom made Joe peer around Kip's head. In front of them, a ten-foot section of track suddenly collapsed with a rumbling crash.

Joe's eyes widened in horror as concrete and steel crumpled, leaving a gaping hole. The bob-sled tore forward, angling straight for the rubble-filled gap.

Chapter

Three

HANG ON!" Kip screamed, and yanked on the steering ropes.

Joe braced his hands against the insides of the sled as the body-jarring speed threw him right, then left. In seconds they would reach the chasm.

"I'm going to try to jump it!" Kip shouted over his shoulder.

Jump it! Kip's last words plunged into Joe's mind as the bobsled twisted low into the bank, then swung high and shot into the air.

The sled landed with a bone-rattling thud on the other side of the gap. Joe's neck snapped and the front of his helmet whacked against the back of Kip's. The sled angled awkwardly sideways, then flipped. Joe and Kip spilled onto the icy track. Twisting wildly, the bobsled continued down the run, the two boys sliding after it, their arms and legs flailing.

Crack! Joe hit the curved concrete side full force. The blow slowed him, and he dug in his heels, trying to brake. When he finally skidded to a stop near the bottom of the run, he heard people yelling anxiously.

Joe blinked, totally dazed. Sitting up, he pulled off his helmet and goggles, then glanced around, trying to orient himself. Ten feet ahead, Kip had also slid to a stop. He was lying flat on his stomach on the icy track, but when he saw Joe look his way, he gave him a thumbs-up sign. "What a run!" he called.

"Joe!" Frank peered over the concrete side of the track. "Are you all right?"

Joe gave his head and shoulders a shake. "Everything's still attached. You better see if Kip's okay."

Uncle Walt was leaning over the track, trying to help Kip to his feet. Kip scooted to the side, grasped his uncle's hand, and vaulted to the ground. "He's okay," Frank said. "Let me give you a hand."

"Don't need one." Joe crawled to the edge, then lowered himself to the ground. Shana came jogging up.

"You guys are so lucky!" she exclaimed. "If you'd hit that section of track when it exploded . . ." She shuddered.

"Exploded?" Joe walked unsteadily up the hill toward the ruined track.

Frank nodded. "With a huge boom."

"Fortunately, none of the crew was working here," Shana said as she stopped beside Joe to stare at the mess. Several other construction workers were standing around, shaking their heads. The twisted metal and crumpled concrete reminded Joe of photos he'd seen of destroyed highways after earthquakes.

Stepping around the rubble, Shana pointed to one of the concrete pilings that held up the track. All that was left was a six-inch base of cement with a foot-long pole of metal rebar sticking out of it.

"This *was* a support post," Shana explained, kneeling.

"And it was blown up?" Joe asked, crouching next to her.

"Looks like it. See the black lines scorched into the cement? It's as if dynamite was set right here."

"Hey! Get away from there!"

Joe looked over his shoulder. An older man wearing coveralls, galoshes, and a ski cap hurried out from a trailer fifty feet from them. Uncle Walt rolled his eyes. "Great, it's Weems. Just what we need."

"Get away from there," Roger Weems called to them. "It's dangerous, and you could be destroying valuable evidence."

Joe stood up. "Hello, Mr. Weems," he said, thrusting out his hand. "Joe Hardy reporting for security crew duty."

Weems glanced at Joe's outstretched hand, then at his Lycra outfit. "You're *who?*"

"Joe Hardy, and this is my brother, Frank." Joe put one arm around Frank's shoulder and pushed him forward. "Lucky for you we were on the job. We've already discovered the cause of the explosion. At least, Ms. Cole did."

Shana stood up. "Looks like dynamite."

Uncle Walt nodded in agreement, then ran his fingers through his gray hair. His brow was furrowed with worry lines. "Seems my company hasn't been exempt from the sabotage after all."

Weems pursed his lips peevishly. "Well, thank you all for your input. But my crew, *not* two new guards, will assess the situation, then write a report to the police and the Building and Games Committee."

"And while your inept bunch is muddling around here and writing that report," Uncle Walt said, stepping closer and thrusting his face in Weems's, "someone just might blow up the rest of the place."

"Mr. Weems." Joe inserted himself between Weems and Cole. "My brother and I have a suggestion about security at the gate."

"Security at the gate. What a novel idea. We already have security at the gate," a man added sarcastically.

Joe and the others turned to see the speaker, a good-looking man dressed in a wool overcoat striding toward them. He was flanked by two men wearing dark suits, their barrel-size chests straining their jacket buttons and their thick necks puffing out over their shirt collars. A limousine was parked behind all three.

"That's Horst Kreig," Shana whispered in Joe's ear. "Head of American Progress. He's either building or financing most of the construction for the Sports Park."

"So that's why he's so mad," Joe whispered back.

"We need to keep those environmental crazies away from here," the man continued, his voice rising as he waved his arms dramatically.

Mr. Weems bustled forward. "Mr. Kreig! My crew has been busy, and we've already assessed the situation." He glanced over at Joe and Frank. "Someone dynamited the support columns."

Mr. Kreig shook his head, a disgusted expression on his face. "Great. More delays. Weems, you'd better find out what's going on."

Joe assessed Horst Kreig. He was a handsome man in his fifties, with a straight posture and commanding attitude. When he spoke, everybody stood at attention.

"Glad to see you, Horst." Uncle Walt shook Horst Kreig's hand heartily. Joe was glad to see that Kip's uncle didn't seem the least bit fazed by

Mr. Kreig's importance. "This situation is getting out of hand. Something has got to be done."

Frank stepped up to Mr. Kreig. "We understand that there is a security guard at the main gate, but security needs to be increased. Maybe even round-the-clock guards posted throughout the park."

Mr. Kreig nodded approvingly. "Good suggestion. I take it he's on your crew, Weems. Let's do what he says." He checked his watch. "I want a report by this afternoon," he added, and he headed off.

Joe followed him, careful to sidestep his bodyguards. "Sir, what do you mean by 'those environmental crazies'? Do you have proof they're involved?"

Kreig turned impatiently. "Didn't you read the headlines of this morning's paper, son?"

Joe started. Had he and Frank missed something important?

"Uh, no, sir."

Kreig halted at the limousine. One of the guards opened the back door.

"Then you'd better," he barked as he climbed into the limousine.

Before Joe could ask anything more, the gorilla-necked guy slammed the door, shot Joe a get-lost look, then went around to the driver's side. As the limousine left, Joe shivered.

"What was that all about?" Frank asked, moving up behind his brother.

"I'm not sure, but I think the morning paper will tell us." Gesturing at Frank to join him, Joe took off for the trailer to search for one.

"Morning paper?" Frank repeated when they got inside. Joe nodded as he hurried to the back room where he and Kip had changed. He picked up the paper and read the headline out loud.

"Listen to this, Frank. 'Radical Environmentalist Threatening Sports Park.'"

Frank's eyes widened. "What?"

Joe skimmed the article, reading as he went. "'Tyler Conklin—a member of Earth at All Costs, an eco-terrorist group—is sought in connection with a threatening letter that was sent to the American Progress offices. Details of the letter were not disclosed. However, an interview with Horst Kreig, president of the company, revealed that the Sports Park, home of the Utah Winter Games and the 2002 Olympics, may be the target of the radical environmental group.'"

Joe glanced up. "What do you think of that?"

Frank let out a low whistle. "Earth at All Costs. Never heard of them, but I think we may have just found our saboteurs!"

"He didn't do it," Allison insisted, her eyes flashing. She was slumped on the couch, the newspaper open in her lap. "I don't care what the paper says."

George and Nancy had just finished eating breakfast. After a late night spent calling everyone Allison knew to locate Tyler, George and Nancy had slept in. But from the gray shadows under Allison's eyes, Nancy knew her friend hadn't gotten much sleep.

Nancy sat on the couch opposite Allison. "We believe you. Still, we have to prove it. Which means you have to help us."

Allison's shoulders sagged and her anger seemed to drain away. "I don't know what else to tell you, except that Tyler's sweet and romantic and funny and . . ." Her voice broke.

"But he did belong to Earth at All Costs," George reminded her gently. Sitting on the arm of the couch, she patted her friend's shoulder. "And that's what the police are going to focus on—not his personality."

"But I told that detective he quit the group," Allison said. "He did it as soon as he realized what nuts they were."

Nancy blew out a breath with a whoosh. She knew her friend was stubborn. Still . . . "Didn't you tell me he was a member for a *year?* That's a long time."

"He stayed because he was dating Robyn," Allison muttered. "And—all right, I'll admit it—at first he thought violence was the only way to keep big business and greedy government from ruining our earth. But he changed his opinion, and that's the truth."

George shot Nancy a doubtful look. Frustrated, Nancy ran her fingers through her hair.

Not only was their skiing vacation not turning out as planned, but, despite Allison's protests, Tyler Conklin did sound guilty. Not that she was going to tell Allison that.

Nancy stood up. "Well, sitting around here isn't going to do Tyler any good. If we're going to prove he's innocent, we need to get to work."

Allison brushed the paper off her lap, a hopeful expression on her face. "That sounds great."

"What do you have in mind, Nan?" George asked.

Nancy grabbed her coat off the back of an armchair. "Let's head to Tyler's apartment and check it out. Maybe the police missed something."

Twenty minutes later Nancy and Allison were walking up the steps of the brownstone.

"That was a good idea, leaving George in the car as lookout," Allison said. After digging in her purse, she found the key to Tyler's apartment. Before unlocking the door, she gave Nancy an apologetic grin. "I'm glad you and George are here, Nancy. And I'm sorry things got so messed up."

Nancy squeezed her friend's arm. "Hey, I'm glad we're here to help, too."

Allison opened the door, and she and Nancy walked in. The small apartment was cold, dark, and silent.

"It doesn't look as if he's been back," Allison said dejectedly.

"Which is just as well, since the police are searching for him." Nancy moved slowly around the small living-room area. Since the only window faced the front, she'd be able to hear George signal with a honk if someone else pulled up.

"I want you to go from room to room and look at everything," Nancy told Allison. *Everything. If someone is framing Tyler, he must have been here before. He had to know that Tyler had been a part of Earth at All Costs."

"And how to forge his signature," Allison added, her gaze darting around the living room.

"Also, look for any clue as to where he might be."

Just then a loud honk made Nancy freeze. "That's George!" she gasped. "And she wouldn't signal unless—" A clunk from outside the apartment door made her stop in midsentence. She spun around, her gaze riveted on the door.

Somebody was coming in!

Chapter

Four

"**H**IDE!" Nancy swung around, frantically hunting for somewhere to hide in the tiny efficiency.

"In here." Allison ran into the bedroom. After dropping down on all fours, she wiggled under the bed.

As Nancy crawled in after her, she could hear the front door open. A man began to talk. Nancy held her breath, trying to hear what he was saying.

"It's got to be here somewhere," the man with the deep voice said. "You look in the kitchen. I'll check out the other room."

The squeak of rubber soles on the wood floor grew louder, and someone entered the bedroom. From her hiding place, Nancy could see the man's creased pants legs and polished wing tip shoes. It looked as if he were dressed for business. Drawers thudded open and closed, and clothes fell to the floor. He was obviously going through everything and didn't care if he made a mess.

But what was he looking for?

"The police must have searched the place pretty thoroughly," the second man said as he moved into the bedroom. He wore muddy work-boots and khakis. Black dirt clung to the soles of his shoes and left marks on the floor.

"Which means it mustn't be here, or the cops would have wanted to talk to me already." The first man's voice was gruff and impatient. Obviously, Tyler must have something the man wanted. But what? And why was it so important?

Suddenly Allison started to sniffle. Nancy couldn't turn her head to see what was going on, but she had a good idea. The dust under the bed was an inch thick.

"Look, Mr. Pavin—"

Pavin. Nancy repeated the name in her head.

"I think we better get out of here." The man sounded nervous. "If the cops catch us snooping around, they'll want to talk to us—both of us."

"You're right. Besides, Conklin may be smarter than we think. Too smart to hide it here in his apartment. Let's go."

The two men left. When the apartment door

was closed, Nancy let out a sigh of relief. Allison let out a huge sneeze.

"Ahhhchew!" The sound rang out through the entire small apartment. Nancy tensed, wondering if the men had heard, but when the door didn't open again, she started to giggle.

"Let me out of here," Allison exclaimed, another sneeze erupting. When the two girls crawled out and faced each other, they both started to laugh. From head to toe, they were covered with dust. Pulling a tissue from the box on the bedside stand, Nancy wiped off her face. When she glanced around the room, she realized that every drawer was open and Tyler's belongings were scattered everywhere.

"Yuck." Bending, Allison brushed at her pants and shirt. "I never knew Tyler was such a crummy housekeeper." She glanced over at Nancy. "I wonder who those creeps were."

"I heard the name Pavin when you were trying not to sneeze."

"Pavin!" Allison stood upright. "You mean State Senator Alexander Pavin?"

Nancy stopped wiping her face. "A state senator's name is Pavin? But what would he want with Tyler?"

"Good question." Allison was silent for a moment. "Rumors have dogged Pavin ever since he was elected."

"What kind of rumors?"

"That he accepted illegal campaign contributions. Now he's pushing for a land-swap deal with American Progress, the same company that Tyler supposedly threatened. The deal could be worth a fortune to American Progress."

"And what would Pavin get out of it?" Nancy asked.

Allison shrugged. "I don't know. I only know that the group Tyler and I belong to, Peace on Earth, is mad because part of the land involved in the swap is a quarter-million acres of protected wilderness above Park City. American Progress wants to develop it as a high-priced resort. They claim the resort will bring hundreds of jobs to the people of Utah, as well as millions in revenue. You know, the same old argument: We'll ruin the land by developing it, but look what you'll get in return."

"Hmmm. That's all interesting, but what could Tyler have that Pavin wants?"

Allison shook her head, then smiled mischievously. "But I do know where it might be hidden."

"What!" Nancy exclaimed.

"When we were under the bed, I remembered a conversation Tyler and I once had about Pavin. He said that he wished Pavin would read the book *Earth, Our Greatest Treasure.* He said that then Pavin might understand that greed ruins everything." Nancy must have looked puzzled, because Allison went on. "Then Tyler started laughing as if it was some private joke."

"Like maybe something might be hidden in the book!" Nancy guessed.

"Right." Allison and Nancy went back into the living room to a bookshelf crammed with notebooks, texts, and paperbacks. "I'll start at the top."

Crouching, Nancy skimmed the titles of the row of paperbacks on the bottom shelf. She was checking out an upside-down book when a honk from outside made her jump.

Allison glanced down at the same time Nancy looked up. "Somebody else is coming!" they chorused.

Jumping up, Nancy raced into the bedroom, diving under the bed after Allison. She waited, her heart racing as the doorknob was rattled noisily.

This time they might not be so lucky.

Frank opened the apartment door and peered inside. Breaking and entering was always risky, but they'd just come from the police station where a Detective Urich had refused to tell them anything. That meant they had to check out Tyler Conklin on their own.

Beside him, Joe stuck his lock-picking equipment back in his pocket. "Anybody home?" he whispered.

"No. But it looks like someone beat us to it." Frank surveyed the messy apartment. "The cops aren't usually this destructive."

"Speaking of cops," Joe said, "what if they show up?"

"Then we revert to our security guard roles," Frank replied as he stepped inside. "We'll tell them Weems sent us to check the place out."

Joe chuckled. "Good idea. Blame it on that guy. He sure did hightail it out of the Sports Park when Kreig left."

"Lucky he did. Otherwise we wouldn't have been able to leave." Moving slowly around the room, Frank searched high and low for some clue as to why Tyler Conklin might want to sabotage the Sports Park. Only, he knew that if there had been any clues, there was a good chance they had been snatched.

"Just remember, if we see Conklin, I get first whacks." Joe smacked his fist against his palm. "That explosion he rigged to blow up the bobsled run might have been the last sound I ever heard."

Frank frowned at his brother. "Aren't you being a little hasty? You know, innocent until proven guilty."

"After what I read in the paper, I think he sounds plenty guilty. We need to find him before he blows up something else."

Frank lifted a picture off the wall and checked the back. "Only my hunch is he's not in it alone. Probably that whole organization, Earth at All Costs, is involved."

"Sounds like we should visit them next," Joe said, checking under the sofa.

"I think that's—"

A loud sneeze interrupted Frank's sentence. He spun toward the bedroom. Joe was turned, too, and staring in the same direction. "Conklin?" Joe mouthed silently.

Frank shrugged, then gestured for Joe to follow him. After grabbing a baseball bat that had been leaning against the bookshelf, Joe silently crept up beside him.

As he slowly approached the bedroom, Frank balled his hands into fists. Someone was in there, hiding. Was it Conklin? Would he give them a fight?

When he peered into the bedroom, he first saw the mess—clothes strewn everywhere—then noticed there wasn't any place to hide except . . .

Frank pointed under the bed. Joe nodded and went around to the far side of the bed. When they were both in position, Frank growled, "All right, we know you're under there. Come . . . *owwwwt!*" He let out a cry as someone sank their teeth into his ankle.

Frank jerked his leg and hopped backward. A hand snaked out and grabbed his other ankle, and he fell, landing hard against the chest of drawers. At the same time, someone scrambled out from under the bed. Frank lunged, tackling the person around the legs.

They both fell in a heap on the bedroom floor, Frank on top. Angrily, Frank pinned the person facedown on the floor. A wave of reddish blond hair cascaded over the person's cheek, blocking his view of the face. Still, he could tell by the build that it was a girl. A girl who was giving him one heck of a fight!

"Knock it off," he shouted as he pressed her cheek hard against the floor.

"Get off me, you creep," the girl grunted.

"Only if you'll quit fighting. I'm not going to hurt you."

The girl quit struggling. Eyeing her cautiously, Frank raised himself. The girl had been gasping for breath under his weight.

"Are you okay?"

She nodded, then blew the hair from her cheek. A blue eye glared up at him. Frank was startled. *"Nancy?"*

"Frank?"

Frank jumped off Nancy just as Joe came over, holding the wrist of a tall girl with brown hair. "Let go of me, you caveman!" the girl was shouting. When she saw Nancy on the floor, she jerked her wrist from Joe's grasp and screamed, "You killed her!"

"Nancy, what are you doing here?" Frank put his hand on her shoulder. With a grimace, Nancy rolled onto her side, then sat up.

"What are *you* doing here?" she countered.

"You mean, you know these cretins?" the tall girl exclaimed.

Nancy nodded, then sneezed. Frank started to laugh.

She glared at him. "What's so funny?"

"I should have known it was you. Nobody else could have gotten the better of me like that." Reaching out, he wiped his finger down her cheek. "Plus I'm laughing because you look like a dust mop."

Nancy sneezed again, then said, "Allison Fernley, meet Joe and Frank Hardy."

Allison's mouth fell open. *"The* Joe and Frank? Your friends the detectives?"

Joe stuck out his hand and shook hers. "In the flesh."

Allison pulled her hand from his. "And what are you doing in Tyler's apartment?" she asked suspiciously.

"Good question." Nancy cocked one brow at Frank.

"Uh . . ." Frank wasn't sure how much to tell Nancy, especially in front of her friend. "It's a long story. What are *you* doing here?"

"Skiing," Nancy said.

Joe glanced around. "Not much snow in here."

"No, I mean that's why we're in Utah. Allison's a student at the university. Why are *you* in Utah?"

"We're working with the security crew at the Sports Park," Frank explained.

"The Sports Park, huh?" Nancy nodded knowingly. "That means you must be on a case. Checking out the recent sabotage?"

Before Frank could say anything, Allison jumped in his face. "And you think Tyler's behind it, right?"

"Well, the newspaper did say—"

Allison pointed toward the apartment door. She was flushed and furious. "In that case, I want you out of here. Out!"

Startled by her outburst, Frank stepped backward. "All right, we're going." Joe was already edging toward the door.

Frank shot one last glance at Nancy. He was dying to know what she and Allison had to do with Tyler Conklin, but it was obvious he wasn't going to get any answers now.

Nancy stood up. "I'll walk you two out," she said. When they got outside the apartment, she gave Frank a quick hug. "Sorry about that. Allison's like a lioness protecting her young."

"Do you have any idea what's going on?" Joe asked.

Nancy shook her head. "All we know is that Tyler's being accused and that he's disappeared. But if I find out anything more, I'll let you know."

Frank gave Nancy their phone number at Kip's before she went back into the apartment. After she shut the door, Joe said, "Do you think she's telling us everything?"

Frank shook his head. "No, but I think it's because she's protecting her friend. So if we want to solve our case, it looks like we'll have to do it on our own."

When Frank and Joe had gone, Nancy leaned wearily against the door. She hated not telling them everything, but she knew she couldn't. She'd promised to help Allison find out the truth, which meant she couldn't be swayed by the Hardys' investigation.

Allison was standing at the bookshelf, rummaging furiously through the shelves. "I found it!" She whirled around, holding up a book.

Nancy hurried over. Opening the book, Allison leafed through the pages. A piece of folded paper fell to the floor.

Nancy picked it up. It was a computer printout of names, phone numbers, and financial entries. As Nancy read through it, she noted that Pavin's name was repeated often.

"Bingo." Grinning triumphantly, she handed the printout to Allison. "I think we just found what Senator Pavin was looking for. Now, if we can figure out *why* these names and numbers are so important, we might be able to help Tyler."

Chapter

Five

WHEN NANCY and Allison came out of the brownstone, George flew from the car, an anxious expression on her face. Nancy had never seen her usually calm friend so worked up.

"I thought you guys were never going to come out!" George cried. "I didn't know if you'd been tied up, gagged, or *shot.*"

"Worse," Nancy said, her voice grim. "We were dusted."

George stopped in her tracks. "Dusted? Is that some kind of torture?"

Allison laughed. "Nancy's just teasing. We had to hide under the bed. Tyler's a lousy housekeeper. We were attacked by dust balls."

"I'm just glad you didn't get caught!" George heaved a sigh of relief.

"Well, that's not exactly true," Nancy said as she walked to the car. "Joe and Frank caught us."

Behind her, George exclaimed, "Joe and Frank *Hardy?*"

Nancy had to laugh. "Yeah. I'm surprised you didn't recognize them, Detective Fayne."

"Well, I . . ." George shrugged. "As those first two guys were leaving, I decided I'd better get the license-plate number of any car or truck that stopped at that building. I was trying to read it as the second car pulled up."

"License plate?" Nancy hugged George. "Good work! Now maybe we can learn the identity of the guy with Pavin."

George frowned. "Don't thank me yet," she said. "All I know is that they were driving a pickup truck. The license plate was artfully covered in mud. I couldn't read anything. And the pickup had nothing distinguishing about it."

"At least you tried," Allison said, patting George on the shoulder.

Nancy opened the car door and climbed into the backseat, eager to study the computer printout. If Senator Pavin wanted it so badly, there had to be something incriminating on it.

But what? And why did Tyler have it, and how had he gotten it?

"Where to now?" George asked as she slipped in the front seat. "Lunch, I hope. This surveillance has made me hungry as a bear."

"Lunch!" Allison strapped on her seat belt,

45

then started up the car. "We don't have time for lunch." She revved the motor and zoomed away from the curb so fast, Nancy was thrown back against her seat. "I'm going to introduce you to some eco-terrorists!"

"No question, this is a top-flight facility," Joe Hardy said to Harmon Wilson, the construction foreman for the new outdoor speed-skating oval. "The ice sheet looks perfect against the backdrop of mountains."

Joe stood with Mr. Wilson beside the 400-meter track located in Provo, Utah, some forty minutes south of Salt Lake City. Since the track had recently been sabotaged, the two Hardys wanted to check out the damage, as well as hunt for clues.

Over by a burning pile of lumber, Frank was talking to several construction workers, hoping one of them might have seen something suspicious. Joe's job was to interview the foreman. He'd caught Wilson just as he was leaving for lunch. Already, he'd discovered that Wilson was foreman for a company owned by Horst Kreig called Progress Development, which was part of American Progress.

"The rink is a great facility," Wilson agreed, but the expression in his eyes was troubled. "Since we're near Brigham Young University, it'll get lots of use, even after the Olympics. Now, if we can just finish it without any more problems."

Joe stared at the far end of the track. A section of wall and a chunk of flooring were missing. "You know for sure that it wasn't an accident?"

Wilson nodded. "Oh, yeah. Fortunately, it happened at night so no one was hurt. Unfortunately, that meant no one saw who did it."

"Security is working on that. We're going to start posting round-the-clock guards at all the sports facility sites."

"Good." Wilson eyed Joe. "Aren't you a little young to be working security?"

Joe smiled confidently. "Young and eager." He pulled a pad from his pocket. "Can you tell me the name of anyone you might suspect?"

"I already told Weems and the police," Wilson said impatiently.

"We like to be thorough. Plus you never know when you might remember something important."

Unbuttoning the neck of his workcoat, Wilson leaned against his truck door. "Todd Ellman. He's got a big beef with everybody involved with the Sports Park."

"Todd Ellman?" Joe's voice rose excitedly. "What's he got against the Sports Park?"

"Ellman owned an excavation company. When all this Olympic hoopla got started, he started bragging that his company was going to do all the excavating, which for a project this size meant years of work and great money. He even went out and bought new equipment—graders, dozers. Must have cost hundreds of thousands."

"What happened?"

"He didn't get the contract. It bankrupted him."

Joe whistled. "He must have been mad."

"Right. And you don't want to get Todd Ellman mad."

Joe raised one brow. "Oh?"

"Because he's an explosives expert. And those jobs have been professional, the work of a guy who can blow up anything, anywhere, anytime. And that's Todd Ellman."

"Thanks for the lead." Joe closed his pad. "What's your theory on the local environmentalist groups? The paper seems to be suggesting one of them is behind the sabotage."

With a shrug, Wilson opened the door of his truck. "My experience has been that environmental groups are hardly subversive. They want everybody in the world to know what they're doing and why."

"Like this Tyler Conklin guy who sent the letter to American Progress," Joe prompted.

"Right. Usually it's not just one eco-terrorist. It's a whole crowd of ex-hippie lunatics throwing themselves in front of bulldozers or wrecking dams with carjacks." He snorted. "Bunch of crazies."

"Right," Joe agreed halfheartedly. He wasn't

sure which side he was on. The construction plans for the Sports Park *were* awesome, but at the same time, huge tracts of land and hundreds of trees were being turned into parking lots and buildings.

After Wilson left, Joe spotted his brother heading toward him, a grin on his face.

"What did you find out?" Joe asked him.

"Todd Ellman," Frank said. "Most of the crew agree he's got the expertise and the motive."

Joe fell into step beside his brother. "Wilson said the same thing. Also, he said the company building the track is owned by Horst Kreig and American Progress, Tyler Conklin's enemy."

Frank checked his watch. "Speaking of Conklin, we're supposed to pick up Kip and go to that environmental rally. I want to see if we can find out anything more about our disappearing suspect."

"And find out more about Earth at All Costs," Joe said when they reached Kip's Jeep. Kip had stayed behind at the Sports Park to work with his uncle, who was hurrying to fix the bobsled run before the official dedication on Saturday. "The way Kreig and the other developers talk, the members of Earth at All Costs are a bunch of rabid dogs. I'm kind of eager to meet them!"

Forty minutes later Joe, Kip, and Frank were headed up the sidewalk to the auditorium of a run-down high school.

"This neighborhood looks pretty rough," Joe commented as he glanced around at the older apartment houses and boarded-up stores.

Kip chuckled. "The beautiful people aren't exactly dying to have a bunch of radical environmentalists meet next to their half-a-million-dollar mansions."

"Never thought of it that way," Joe said. He and Frank followed Kip up the steps of the school. Inside, a tall man with a scraggly beard put a hand on Kip's arm to stop him from entering. "No new faces without prior clearance, Coles," he said, eyeing the Hardys suspiciously.

"I know, J.T.," Kip said in a smooth voice. "But these are old friends. Remember I told you about my adventures in the desert?" Kip grinned proudly at Joe and Frank. "These were the two detectives who were with me."

J.T.'s eyes lit up, and he shook Joe and Frank's hands heartily. "Hey, nice to meet ya! Anyone who can handle an ex-con armed with bazookas and grenades is all right. Go on in." Slapping Joe and then Frank on the back, he ushered them into the auditorium.

"Bazookas and grenades?" Joe murmured to Kip. "Wasn't that a bit of an exaggeration?"

His friend chuckled. "Well, the story has gotten a little wilder as it's been passed along."

The auditorium was half filled; Joe quickly estimated between eighty and ninety people. At the front of the stage a podium had been set up, and a woman was speaking to the audience. Joe glanced at Frank, who gave him a surprised look in return. Neither Hardy had realized that the Earth at All Costs group would be this large.

Kip led them to a half-empty row near the front. The speaker, a petite woman with bushy blond hair held back with a hairband, was talking about a rally she'd recently attended in Washington, D.C. To her left, a man and a woman sat behind a long table. The woman wore several "Save the Earth" buttons pinned to the front of her blouse. The man was bald and pale and wore a suitcoat.

"These are the wild radicals?" Joe whispered to Frank and Kip.

"When I came home from the rally, I realized EAAC was not doing all it could," the woman speaker said loudly. "The construction of the Sports Park is out of control. And despite our letters and petitions to our state legislature, Utah continues to support big business and development. I say it's time we joined Tyler in more radical measures."

Tyler? The name caught Joe's attention. Leaning sideways, he whispered to Kip, "Is she talking about Tyler Conklin?"

"Probably," Kip whispered in turn. "That's Robyn Bickmore, president of EAAC. She and Tyler were pretty serious a couple of months ago.

But then Tyler split with the group. Last I heard, he was dating some student on campus and had joined the university group Peace on Earth."

Joe chuckled. "We met the girl he's dating. Quite a wildcat."

"Peace on Earth?" Frank repeated from the seat on the other side of Kip. "They don't sound too radical."

"They aren't. That's why I'm not sure what Robyn's talking about. I thought it was understood by EAAC that Tyler was no longer in agreement with their methods."

"Then why did he send that threatening letter to American Progress?" Joe asked.

Kip put a finger to his lips. "Let's listen and find out."

Joe turned his attention back to the woman. She was a compelling speaker, and he could see why she was the president. But so far the rally was as tame as a PTA meeting.

"Wait a minute." A man a few aisles ahead of Joe stood up and addressed Robyn. "Conklin isn't with us anymore. Why are we supporting him?"

Robyn smiled confidently at the man. "Tyler only *told* us he wasn't part of our group. I have proof that he pretended to leave EAAC to pull the wool over the eyes of the officials. That way, when he sabotaged the Sports Park, it would turn the authorities' attention away from EAAC."

"Liar!"

Joe twisted to scan the auditorium to locate the woman who had yelled out. Seconds later Allison Fernley appeared in the aisle with Nancy and George behind her.

Allison stopped halfway down the aisle. "Tyler had nothing to do with the explosions, and you know it!"

Robyn smirked. "Oh, really?" She held up a letter and waved it at the audience. "Then why did he write EAAC, stating that he'd been planning this subversive attack all along?"

"No way!" Red faced with fury, Allison glanced around the auditorium. "Tyler is a member of Peace on Earth. He would never use violent methods."

A buzz of conversation broke through the audience. Leaning over the microphone, Robyn called them to order. "Members, I would like to introduce you to Allison Fernley. You see, Tyler used Allison as he used Peace on Earth, as a means to an end. And his end is to stop construction of the Sports Park!" Raising her fist, she punched the air. "Are we with him?"

"Yes!"

"No!" Allison barreled down the aisle, her eyes stormy. "I don't believe you. Tyler didn't write that letter."

As Allison hurried toward Robyn, the other woman speaker rose from her seat at the table to confront her. Nancy and George hustled to Allison's side at the same time that several guys surged from the front row to flank Robyn protectively.

Worried that someone was going to get hurt, Joe shot up from his seat. "Looks like trouble, guys," he said in a low voice. Frank and Kip were already trying to push their way down the crowded aisle.

Jumping over the row of seats in front of him, Joe went to help Nancy. When he reached the podium, Nancy shot Joe a surprised, then grateful, look.

"Give me that letter," Allison demanded. "I want to see for myself that Tyler wrote it."

"Allison, let's go," Nancy said above the noise and confusion. "We can meet with Robyn later."

"There's no reason for me to meet with you—*ever*," Robyn retorted. "Tyler's behind these explosions. I know. I taught him how to use dynamite." She grinned nastily. "And don't be hurt, Allison. After all, Tyler used you for a good cause."

Allison scowled. "You're lying. I bet you're behind those explosions, only you're too chicken to admit it, so you're blaming them on Tyler!" Reaching out, she snatched at the letter still in Robyn's hand.

"Hey, watch it, lady." A tall skinny guy with a hawklike nose grabbed Allison by the arm and began to pull her backward.

"Let her go!" Nancy protested.

A second guy wearing a baseball cap stepped in

front of her. "We will. After we throw you both out." Slapping an arm around Nancy's shoulder, he spun her toward the exit.

That was too much for Joe. "Excuse me," he said politely. "But if you let my friends go, I'm sure they'll leave peacefully."

"Oh, they'll leave, all right," Hawk Nose said. "And so will you!"

"Only when I'm ready," Joe shot back.

"Joe!"

Joe glanced over his shoulder. Frank and Kip had broken through the crowd and were heading toward them.

Good, reinforcements, Joe thought. When he turned to face the guy in the baseball cap, he was just in time to see the man cock his arm back, ready to swing. "Then get ready," the guy sneered.

"Watch out, Joe!" Nancy shrieked.

Joe ducked sideways, but he was too late. A fist landed on his jaw, pain exploding in his head. He dropped to the floor like a sack of potatoes.

Chapter

Six

NANCY FELL to her knees beside Joe. "Are you all right?"

Joe's face was white as he struggled to a sitting position and growled, "Let me at that gorilla."

"Come on, lady." The guy in the baseball cap jerked Nancy to her feet. Two other guys hoisted up Joe under his armpits.

As the guy propelled Nancy up the aisle, she looked around frantically for George and Allison. An angry voice rang out from the back of the auditorium, where Allison and George were being escorted out the door. Behind them, several EAAC members had Frank and another guy in tow.

"Let's get the last of these troublemakers out of here," the guy in the baseball cap said to the two men pushing and dragging Joe up the aisle.

Nancy saw Joe wince with pain. Angrily, she jerked her arm from her captor's grasp. "I can walk, thank you," she told him. He scowled but didn't take hold of her again. After making sure Joe was okay, Nancy hurried after the others. When she got outside, Allison was talking to the guy who'd been with Frank, while George and Frank paced anxiously on the sidewalk.

"Nancy!" When he saw her, Frank vaulted up the steps. A big guy with a hairy beard immediately blocked the doorway.

Quickly, Nancy reassured Frank that Joe was okay. "He's going to have a monster of a headache, though."

Joe stumbled out the door and onto the landing. The guy with the beard shot them all nasty looks, then turned and went back inside the auditorium, slamming the door behind him.

"Hey, guys!" Joe greeted merrily. "Some party!" He swayed unsteadily, then plopped down on the top step.

Nancy went to sit next to him. Gently, she put her hand on his chin and turned his head toward her. His jaw was already turning black and blue. "We'd better get you some ice."

"What in the world happened in there?" Frank asked, sitting on Joe's other side.

"I'll tell you what happened." Allison strode

to the bottom step and looked up at them. "Robyn Bickmore is a big fat liar who's trying to get Tyler in trouble."

"Now wait a minute, Allison." Frank's friend came over and stood next to her.

"Kip Coles, meet Nancy Drew and George Fayne," Frank said. "I guess you know Allison," he said to Kip.

Kip nodded. "We met at a couple of rallies." He turned to face her. Nancy could tell by Allison's expression that no matter what Kip said, she would refuse to believe that Tyler was guilty of the sabotage. "Robyn doesn't usually lie. And according to the newspaper, Tyler did send that threatening letter to American Progress."

"He didn't." Allison crossed her arms and glared at him.

"I've known Tyler for a while," Kip went on. "And I know how passionate he is about the environment. Like you, I don't think he's responsible for blowing up facilities at the Sports Park," he added quickly before Allison could protest. "But I do believe he'd take credit if he thought it would put a stop to the development."

Allison cocked her head. Nancy thought Frank's friend had an interesting theory. After all, according to the paper, several acts of sabotage had taken place before the threatening letter was sent to American Progress. Maybe Tyler was just using the explosions to his—and EAAC's—advantage.

"That would make sense *if* Tyler was the type of person even to think about blowing things up," Allison said slowly. "And maybe he was, once. But not anymore."

"Can you prove it?" Frank asked.

For a second Allison chewed on her lip. Finally she said, "Maybe some of the members of Peace on Earth could tell you what Tyler's like now. There's a meeting tomorrow."

"No way," Joe said. He was holding his head in his hands. "I'm never going to another environmental group meeting in my life."

"Really." George shuddered. "That wasn't my idea of fun, either."

"Only I've got to talk to Robyn again," Allison declared. "I've got to get a look at that letter. There's no way Tyler could have written it."

Nancy rolled her eyes. Allison was as stubborn as a mule.

"I bet Robyn and her friends will be at the rave party tonight," Kip suggested.

"Rave?" George asked, coming up next to him. Kip wore jeans and a goosedown vest over a flannel shirt. His face was windburned, his hair tousled, and his build was rugged. Just George's type, Nancy thought with a grin.

"An underground party," Kip explained. "This one's at an old abandoned warehouse on the west side of town."

"We could check it out," Nancy said. "Even if Robyn's not there, we could talk to some of her friends. I'd like to ask them some questions."

"Count me in!" Joe stood up, and Nancy was glad to see some of the old sparkle in his eyes. "I'd like to meet some of her friends again, too. Especially Mr. Baseball Cap," he said, flexing his jaw. "And this time he won't get the jump on me."

"I think I know what the numbers on this computer printout mean," Nancy said excitedly. The three girls were sitting around Allison's small kitchen table, eating lunch.

George lowered the ham sandwich she was about to devour. "What?"

"Bankwire receipt numbers, followed by a date and an amount. And if I'm right, it looks as if Pavin received a lot of money this year in large lump sums."

"But why would Tyler have that information?" Allison asked, putting a slice of whole wheat bread on top of her turkey sandwich.

Nancy shook her head. "I don't know. And why would Pavin want it back? Unless . . ." She glanced sharply at Allison. "You said there were rumors Pavin had accepted illegal campaign contributions before he was elected."

"Right."

"What if some of the contributions were from big businesses who are still paying him off now that he's been elected? In return, Pavin could be backing legislation and finagling deals that would favor them—like this land-swap deal with American Progress."

Allison nodded excitedly. "Makes sense. Pavin always has an environmentally friendly platform but then turns around and favors companies like Progress Development."

"But how would Tyler find out about the payoffs?" Nancy wondered. She picked up her ham and cheese sandwich and absently took a bite.

Allison shook her head. "I don't know. He never talked about investigating Pavin, unless—" She snapped her fingers. "Wait! At the beginning of this semester, Tyler did an internship at city hall. He worked with someone in records—"

"Records!" Nancy's eyes lit up. "He could have had access to the main computer. What if he printed out a bunch of information on Pavin?"

"And discovered those bankwire receipts," George added. "Maybe he didn't know what they were until news of the land-swap deal hit the papers."

"And believe me," Allison said, "Tyler was furious when he read that Pavin was trying to get the state to give that wilderness area in the Wasatch Mountains to American Progress to develop into a resort."

George frowned. "But if the printout does show illegal contributions, why would Pavin have entered them in his computer? That seems so risky."

"Maybe he disguised them as legal contributions," Nancy guessed. "Or maybe he thought his computer files were safe. After all, our nation's defense secrets are kept on computer."

"A good hacker can get into just about any file or system," Allison pointed out.

"Too bad the police took Tyler's computer." Nancy took a swig of her milk and leaned back in her chair. "The only problem is, what does Pavin have to do with a threatening letter sent to American Progress?"

George set her elbows on the table. "Maybe Pavin sent the letter, framing Tyler."

"Right," Allison agreed, a huge smile brightening her face. "If Tyler was discredited in the newspaper as a radical eco-terrorist, no one would believe anything he said about Pavin—even if Tyler had proof."

"It all makes sense, guys," Nancy said. "Only how are *we* going to prove any of it?" She tapped the printout with her forefinger. "I'm sure if we confronted Pavin he'd be able to come up with a logical explanation for the sums listed here."

Allison set her glass down with a bang. "We need to find Tyler! He's the only one who really knows what's on the printout."

Nancy knew Allison was right. There was only one problem: None of them had a clue as to Tyler Conklin's whereabouts.

"All quiet here, Joe," Frank said into his radio. He was checking out the seventy-meter ski jump, now in its final stages of construction. It was ten o'clock at night, and despite Frank's heavy coat, ski cap, and boots, he was freezing on top of the tower.

"Quiet here, too, Frank," Joe responded via radio. Inside the tower, Joe was checking out the second level, where the reception area and observation deck were located. "I'll meet you at the elevator."

That afternoon, Weems had assigned guards to each of the various facilities. Joe and Frank had the five P.M. to eleven P.M. shift at the ski jump. Then they were meeting Nancy and the others at the rave party.

Standing on the top of the ramp, Frank shivered as he looked down the long slope to the landing hill, which was illuminated by several lights from the parking area. For a second, he imagined what it would feel like to zoom down the slick inrun to the take-off point, where he'd sail into the air and fly like a bird—

Clunk! A noise behind Frank made him whirl around. Weems had reminded everybody that the ski jump was the target mentioned in Tyler

Conklin's letter to American Progress. Not that Frank needed to be warned. He already knew the saboteurs meant business.

Stepping closer to the start gates, Frank flicked on his flashlight. "Joe?"

The wind whipped around the tower, rattling some loose boards. Frank heaved a sigh and flicked off his light as a figure dressed in black lunged at him.

Frank froze as he was shoved hard. The force sent Frank flying backward over the edge of the inrun. Landing hard on the ice-covered incline, he flew wildly down the steep slope of the ski jump.

Chapter

Seven

FRANK SLID DOWN the ice-covered incline, his head banging on the hard surface, his arms and legs splayed awkwardly.

"Ahhh!" he screamed, more out of anger than fear. How could he have let someone catch him off guard!

Digging his heels and gloved fingers into the ice, Frank finally slowed to a stop. He had slid about halfway down the inrun. Fortunately, his heavy clothes had kept him from being hurt.

Bracing himself against the two sides to keep from sliding again, Frank sat up and looked at the top of the tower. It was empty and dark. His attacker had fled.

"Frank!"

He glanced around, but he could see nothing.

Who was calling him? Then the voice called his name again, and this time the acompanying static made Frank realize the sound was coming from the radio he'd stuck in his pocket.

He pulled it out. "What?"

"Are you playing around again?" Joe asked.

Frank snorted. "Not exactly."

"Then get down off that ski jump."

Frank's jaw dropped. Where was Joe and how did he know he was on the jump?

"Down here, stupid."

Frank looked over his shoulder to the bottom of the jump. Joe stood on the landing hill, waving his flashlight.

"I thought you were going to meet me at the elevator inside the tower," Frank said into the radio.

"I was," Joe replied. "I waited by the doors. When the elevator went past going down, I got suspicious. So I took the stairs."

Frank's pulse began to race. "You caught the creep who rammed me?"

"Lost him. The guy must have had a snowmobile parked nearby for a quick getaway. I heard it start up, but all I saw were the tracks headed for the woods."

"Rats!" Frank smacked his gloved hand on the ice. "I hope you radioed for backup."

"I told Weems which direction the guy was going."

Frank chuckled. "That means Weems will send a crew in the opposite direction." Frustrated, he blew out his breath. "We're going to have to hunt down the guy ourselves."

"Hey, Frank?" Frank could tell by the teasing tone in Joe's voice that his brother was about to razz him. "You've got an even bigger problem than finding your attacker."

"What's that?" Frank asked cautiously.

"How are you going to get off that ski jump?"

"So, how fast were you going down the ski jump, Frank?" Nancy hollered, trying to make herself heard over the noise of the bass booming from the floor-to-ceiling speakers. On a makeshift stage, the band, a garishly dressed trio, screeched indecipherable lyrics into their microphones while pounding guitars.

"And did you get a good liftoff?" George added, her eyes twinkling. She and Kip stood on the other side of Frank.

Frank shook his head. "Would you guys lay off?"

"No way!" Raising his glass in a toast, Kip declared, "Three cheers for the next Olympic champion ski jumper!"

"Hip, hip, hooray!" chorused the threesome. Just then Joe came up, holding the hand of a tall, cute girl with curly brown hair. "Shana Coles, I want you to meet my friends Nancy and George.

And of course, you've met Frank, the Olympic ski jumper."

Everyone laughed. Standing on tiptoe, Nancy hunted for Allison. Intent on finding Robyn Bickmore, Allison had disappeared into the throng of dancers. Despite the bitter cold outside, the crush of people made the huge, unheated warehouse feel like a furnace.

Caught up in the music, Nancy began to sway. She was almost glad Allison had headed off. After all, the trip to Utah was supposed to be a vacation. An evening away from sleuthing was just what Nancy needed.

"Wanna dance?" she heard Kip ask George. Eagerly, her friend nodded and the two headed off. Joe had already led Shana into the gyrating crowd.

Frank gave Nancy a hesitant look. "Uh, you want to join the natives?"

Nancy laughed. "Actually, I'm feeling guilty for losing Allison. Maybe I had better find her."

"I'll go with you," he said, sounding relieved.

"So, who do you think pushed you down the jump?" Nancy asked as they made their way through the crowd.

"Don't tell Allison, but Weems and his crew are convinced it's Tyler Conklin and the members of EAAC. Conklin did threaten to blow up the ski jump. But when we searched the place, we found no evidence of explosives."

"But who do *you* think it was?" Nancy shouted in Frank's ear.

He shrugged. "Joe and I trailed the snowmobile to a road where we found it abandoned. Tire tracks suggest the rider had a car parked there, or else someone picked him up. Weems is trying to find the owner of the snowmobile, but we figure it was stolen so it couldn't be traced."

Pointing toward an empty corner at the back, Frank steered Nancy out of the crush of bodies. Gratefully, she collapsed against the wall. The area, far from the speakers, was relatively quiet.

"So it *could've* been Conklin at the ski-jump tower," Frank continued. "Tomorrow we're checking out our other lead—that the bomber might be a disgruntled contractor. Since millions are being invested in the Sports Park, there's a lot of money to be made by engineers, builders, etcetera. We know of at least one guy who went bankrupt when he lost a bid on excavating work."

"That might make someone mad enough to blow up the bobsled run," Nancy commented. She wondered how Frank's information tied in with what she was speculating about Pavin. If the senator had received campaign contributions from certain businesses, maybe he had favored those businesses when it came to awarding state contracts.

"Nancy!" Allison pushed her way toward her

friend. Her eyes glittered and she was breathing hard.

Nancy straightened. "What's wrong?"

"I think I know who's got Tyler and where they have him hidden!"

"What!"

Allison glanced nervously over her shoulder. "I finally found Robyn and her henchmen. They didn't see me, so I was able to sneak up behind them and eavesdrop. They were talking about a secret room here in the warehouse."

"What makes you think Tyler's there?" Frank asked.

"Because I heard them say his name." Grabbing Nancy's hand, she pulled her toward an exit.

"Where are we going?"

"To find that room!" Pushing open the door, Allison yanked Nancy outside with her. A shot of cold air shocked them as they stepped into an alley. Nancy was relieved to see that Frank had followed. If she was going on a wild-goose chase, she might need backup.

"What are we doing out here?" Nancy asked, wishing she had her coat.

Leaning back, Allison studied the metal stairs that zigzagged from the roof to the alley. "I already checked the first floor of the warehouse," she said. "And except for the restrooms, it's just one big area."

"No rooms behind the stage?" Frank asked.

Allison shook her head. "That means the hiding place has to be on the second or third floor."

Swallowing hard, Nancy checked out the stairs. They were rusty and swayed in the wind. Frank stuck his hands in his pockets and rocked back on his heels. He didn't look eager to climb them either, though she knew he'd love to confront Tyler Conklin.

"Allison, if you're certain Tyler's here, we should call the police."

Allison looked at Nancy as if she'd suggested doing something crazy. "So they can arrest Tyler? No way. Come on." Grasping the metal railing, Allison started up the steps. "Once we find Tyler, we can clear up this whole mystery."

Nancy gave Frank a pained look. He bowed at the waist. "After you, madam."

"Gee, thanks," she muttered, climbing after Allison.

When they reached the door leading to the second floor, Allison pushed it open. They found themselves in a dark hallway. Stepping around Allison, Frank pulled a flashlight from his back pocket and turned it on.

The light bounced off cobwebs and dust. When Frank aimed the beam along the floor of the hall, Nancy could see scuffmarks in the fallen plaster and dirt. "Someone's been here recently," she said.

"Tyler! I bet they've got him tied up and hidden," Allison said.

Nancy doubted it. Why would members of EAAC want to kidnap Tyler?

"Well, let's take a look," Frank said. Moving slowly down the hall, he peered into the open doorways. "We'll check every room, but then I'm out of here. I've already had my thrills for the night."

Nancy followed Frank, Allison trailing. The music from below was so loud that it made the floorboards vibrate. As they passed each room, Nancy peeked in, not sure what to expect. But except for old newspapers and trash, the rooms were empty.

"Satisfied?" Frank asked.

"No." Allison pointed to the end of the hall. "There's one more place to check."

Frank aimed the light on a big sliding door. "Looks like an old freight elevator."

"And I bet it goes up to the third floor." Grabbing the handle, Allison slid the door open.

"It doesn't look safe," Frank said.

Allison kicked a gum wrapper on the floor of the elevator. "Safe enough for someone else to use. Come on." Stepping inside, she turned to face Nancy and Frank, her hands on her hips as if daring them to follow.

Nancy bowed at the waist. "After you, sir."

Reluctantly, Frank followed Allison inside.

After Nancy went in, she shut the door. Frank flashed the light on the control panel and pressed the button for the third floor. With a loud grinding of gears, the elevator lurched upward.

"It works!" Nancy said, surprised. Minutes later the elevator shuddered to a halt. She grabbed the handle, eager to get out, but when she pulled, nothing happened.

She backed out of the way. "You try it, Frank."

He handed her the flashlight, then yanked on the handle. The door wouldn't budge.

"Come on, guys, quit clowning around." Allison pushed past them. With both hands, she pulled the handle. "It's stuck!" she cried. "We're trapped in here and no one knows where we are!"

"There must be a way out," Nancy reassured her.

Frank swept the beam of light around the top of the elevator. "It looks like there's a hinged door in the ceiling."

"One of us can climb onto the roof of the elevator," Nancy said "then jump into the hall and try to open the door from the other side."

All at once Nancy smelled smoke. Looking down, she noticed a gray cloud curling up from under the door. Nancy put an ear to the door and heard popping and crackling.

"Oh, no!" Nancy exclaimed. "Someone must

have set a fire in the hall right outside the freight elevator."

"A fire!" Allison squealed.

Nancy's heart raced as the smoke swirled around her ankles, covering the floor like ground fog. Whirling, she faced Frank and Allison. "If we don't get out of here, we'll suffocate!"

Chapter

Eight

"We've got to get out of here!" Panicking, Allison grabbed the door handle and yanked, but still it wouldn't budge.

"The panel in the ceiling." Nancy pointed upward. She knew it was best to stay close to the floor, but because the smoke was coming in at floor level they'd have to go out through the ceiling. "It's our only escape."

Frank crouched. "Step up on my leg, Nancy, and see if you can knock the panel out. You'll need to steady her, Allison."

Nancy climbed onto Frank's thigh while Allison held her waist. Using the heel of her hand, she pounded on the door in the ceiling. It was nailed tightly.

Tears caused by smoke and frustration stung

Nancy's eyes. "It's no use." She jumped down. "Maybe if we all pull on the handle."

"And maybe if we shout someone will hear us," Frank suggested as he stood up.

The three tugged hard on the door handle, at the same time hollering at full volume. Nancy doubted that anyone would be on the third floor of a deserted warehouse, and with the band playing, no one downstairs would hear them.

Then Nancy heard someone yell from the other side.

"Quiet!" she shushed.

"Hang on, we'll get you out!" a person shouted, and seconds later, the freight door slid open. On the other side of the door, a pile of newspapers smoldered. A tall guy wearing a baseball cap was dumping a bucket of water on the pile while another stomped on the still-burning ashes. Nancy recognized both of them from the EAAC meeting.

"Jump over the papers!" someone urged. Nancy glanced to her left. Robyn Bickmore was gesturing for them to hurry. She held the handle of a Coleman lantern, which was illuminating the crazy scene.

Allison leaped over the newspapers. Frank grabbed Nancy's hand, and as they jumped together, she couldn't help but wonder what Robyn was doing upstairs. Was Allison right? Did EAAC have Tyler hidden somewhere?

Taking Allison's elbow, Robyn steered her clear of the fire. Angrily, Allison jerked away.

"Where's Tyler?" she demanded.

"So that's why you were snooping," Robyn said. "It's lucky we followed you, or you'd be charcoal-broiled by now."

Allison narrowed her eyes. "Quit acting so innocent, Robyn. I bet you and your goons locked us in that elevator."

Robyn set down the lantern and crossed her arms. "Then why would we let you out?" She pointed to a brick on the floor. "That was wedged in the door handle on this side."

"Maybe you were just trying to scare us," Nancy challenged. "So we wouldn't search the warehouse." She studied Robyn closely.

Obviously, the EAAC president had something to hide, or she wouldn't have followed them.

Arms still crossed, Robyn focused somewhere behind and between Nancy and Allison. By this time, Frank had helped the two guys to stomp out the newspapers. The air smelled like wet ashes, and a gray cloud of smoke filled the hallway.

"You're right, we didn't want you up here on the third floor," Robyn finally said. "But it doesn't have anything to do with Tyler."

"How do we know?" Nancy countered. Frank came up to stand beside her. She knew he was just as interested in finding Tyler.

Robyn pressed her lips together in a firm line. "You'll have to trust me."

"Trust you!" Allison snorted. "After you tried to pass off that forged letter as real!"

"It is real." Sticking her hand in her coat pocket, Robyn pulled out a folded piece of paper and handed it to Allison. "Read it yourself."

Slowly Allison took the letter. When she finished reading, her face was chalk white.

"See?" Robyn scoffed. "I told you it was from Tyler. The letter came to EAAC at the same time American Progress received their threat. I figured Tyler had been planning this for a long time. We often talked about blowing up something at the Sports Park as a way of warning those pigs at Progress Development to quit ruining the environment."

Allison handed the letter to Nancy as if in a daze. Nancy skimmed it quickly, while Frank read it over her shoulder. Robyn had reported the truth at the meeting. According to the letter, Tyler had left EAAC and joined Peace on Earth to throw the police and officials off track.

"That's Tyler's signature?" Nancy asked Allison.

She nodded. Tears were rolling down her cheeks. "Well, there's one good thing," Allison said, her voice cracking. "He didn't say that he was using *me.*"

Robyn snatched the letter from Nancy. "It's

obvious that he was. Otherwise, why would he leave *me* for you?" She jerked her thumb toward the exit door at the end of the hall. "Now we'd like you to leave."

"Not until you tell us what you're hiding up here." Frank stepped so close to Robyn that she had to lean back to see him. Immediately, the two guys flanked her protectively. "I work for the Building and Games Security Committee. We don't take these bombings lightly. If EAAC has anything to do with the sabotage of the Sports Park, then the group is in big trouble."

A momentary spark of fear flickered in Robyn's eyes before she regained her composure. "EAAC has nothing to do with the explosions, except that we support Tyler," she said firmly.

Nancy held her breath as Frank continued to study Robyn. Was she telling the truth? Her words and tone sounded genuine, but Nancy figured the president of a radical organization like EAAC was used to covering herself.

Frank backed off. "Okay. For now. Come on, Nancy, Allison, let's get out of here."

As she strode down the hall with Frank and Allison, Nancy could feel the glares of the three EAAC members. When she reached the door to the outside stairs, she turned and looked at Robyn. The light from the lantern cast sinister shadows across the woman's face. Nancy knew Robyn was hiding something. But what?

Smiling contemptuously, Robyn called, "But that doesn't mean EAAC *won't* get involved." Raising her fist, she punched the air. "So tell the Building and Games Committee to watch out!"

"I can't believe I missed all the excitement last night," Joe said to Frank the next morning. The two Hardys were headed to Todd Ellman's office. "When Shana and I couldn't find you guys, we figured the noise at the rave was too much and you left. We never suspected you were trapped in a burning elevator."

Yawning sleepily—he and Shana hadn't left the party until two A.M.—Joe glanced at his brother. Frank was concentrating on driving the van Weems had lent them. Several inches of snow had fallen since they'd woken up, and the roads were slick.

When the Hardys had reported to work, Frank told Weems all about the EAAC members and their interest in the third floor of the warehouse. Weems immediately called the police, then gathered a team to search the place. Frank had been excited about joining the team, so when Weems instructed the two Hardys to check out Ellman's abandoned office instead, Joe knew his brother had been pretty mad.

"So, you and Shana had a good time last night?" Frank finally asked.

"A great time." Joe smiled, thinking about how much fun he'd had with Shana. Not only was she beautiful and a good dancer, but she knew as much about the outdoors as her cousin. "Kip and George hit it off, too. They talked nonstop about hiking, climbing, kayaking, skiing—you name a sport, they covered it."

Sitting forward, Joe looked out the windshield at the soft snow swirling everywhere. "Talking about skiing, think we'll ever get on the slopes?"

"Not if this case keeps heating up. Though Weems did promise us Thanksgiving Day off."

"Yes!" Joe grinned. "And maybe when we check out Ellman's office, we'll find the same kind of explosives used to blow up the bobsled run. Then we can close this case and have a vacation."

Frank snorted. "Sure, Joe. And maybe Ellman will just turn himself in to the police."

"It'd be nice of him." Joe chuckled. "Hey, there's the sign." He pointed to a faded wooden board with "Ellman Excavating" written on it. A For Sale sign with the realtor's name and number had been stuck in the ground in front of the old company sign. "Turn right."

The van bumped down a rutted gravel road. Ellman's business consisted of a one-story concrete office building and several garage-type structures. A rusty bulldozer and an old dump truck were parked to one side.

Frank pulled the van in front of the building. "Place looks pretty rough."

"Looks like it'll be easy to break into, though,"

Joe said, noticing that one of the windows was already broken.

"Of course. Do you think Weems would send us on a dangerous assignment?" Frank said sarcastically. Climbing from the van, he went up to the front door and tried the knob. "Locked."

Joe headed over to the broken window. While Frank kept watch, he knocked out the rest of the jagged glass. Reaching through, he found the latch and forced the window up. Then he hoisted himself over the ledge and dropped into a dark, empty office. Hands on his hips, Joe surveyed the room. It was paneled in cheap, dark plywood. Stained gold carpet covered the floor. The furniture was gone, but trash and papers were piled everywhere.

Weems had instructed them to find anything that might link Ellman to the explosions. Joe figured a box of dynamite would be nice, or at least blueprints of the Sports Park.

"Do you think this was Ellman's office?" Frank asked when he landed beside Joe.

"Who knows? The building's not that big."

Joe knelt by a stack of folders. He picked one up. Something squeaked and scurried across his fingers, startling him. "Argh!" He jerked his hand away. The folder dropped to the floor, and a stack of half-chewed papers spilled out.

Frank stuck his head around the doorjamb. "You found something?"

"A mouse."

Frank cracked up. "Hey, make sure you interrogate every one of those mice carefully. They could be accomplices." Joe heard him laughing all the way down the hall.

"Real funny," Joe muttered. He wrinkled his nose at the smell. Okay, so detective work wasn't all glamour. But inspecting a mouse nest?

Using the edge of the file folder, he poked through the torn papers. Most were bids for jobs building the Sports Park. They were dated about a year ago. Scooping them up, he shoved them into the folder. He grinned, imagining the look on Weems's face when he handed him the stinky evidence.

"Hey, Joe! I think I've got something!" Jumping up, Joe hurried from the room. Frank was sitting on the edge of an old metal desk in the reception area by the front door. A trash can was perched on the desk. Beside it, Frank had arranged scraps of paper.

"Playing again, Frank?" Joe joked.

"I'm putting a puzzle together."

Joe peered over his brother's shoulder. "A letter from Ellman?"

"Yeah. To some guy named Pavin. It's ripped in a hundred pieces, like someone was really mad or didn't want anyone to see it. The interesting thing is, it's not written on company letterhead. That means it was personal, but the content isn't personal. It has to do with Pavin reneging on a deal."

Joe raised one brow. "A business deal?"

"Sounds like it had to do with excavating some pretty big jobs, though I'm missing a bunch of pieces." Tipping the trash can, Frank went through it once more but found nothing.

"The rest of the letter is probably lining some mouse's nest," Joe said. "Here." He held out the file folder. "Put the pieces in with the other stuff. We can let Weems sort it out."

"I'd like to find out who this Pavin guy is," Frank said.

"I bet Kip will know." Joe checked his watch. "We're supposed to meet him at his uncle's trailer for lunch." Kip had left Park City early to help his uncle's crew repair the bobsled run in time for Saturday's dedication.

Joe grinned—he was meeting Shana for lunch, too—but then forced his mind back to work. "I'd like Uncle Walt to look at the copies of these bids Ellman made for the Sports Park. He might be able to help us figure out if Ellman's our man."

Half an hour later Joe, Kip, Shana, Frank, and Mr. Coles were seated on boxes in the construction trailer. Uncle Walt was slowly chewing a sandwich while he glanced through the folder of bids.

"Pavin, huh?" Kip was saying. He held a steaming thermos of leftover stew, which smelled delicious. Shana was eating a homemade roll stuffed with roast beef. Joe and Frank had stopped off at a fast-food place. By now their burgers and fries were cold.

Kip waved his spoon in the air. "If it's Alex Pavin, he's a state senator. And believe me, he has his hand in every pie—including construction of the Sports Park."

Eagerly, Joe leaned forward, his elbows on his knees. Shana sat close to him, sharing the same box. Even zipped up in heavy coveralls, her hair a mop of windblown curls, she looked gorgeous.

"I wonder if Ellman and Pavin cooked up some sort of deal," Joe said. "That would explain why Ellman was so sure he was going to get the bids for excavating the sites at the Sports Park."

"But according to these letters," Uncle Walt said, "there's no way he should have won the contracts. His bids were all high."

Frank nodded as he stuck a french fry in his mouth. "Maybe Ellman figured he and Pavin had a deal no matter what. Then Pavin double-crossed him."

Just then the sound of the front door of the trailer banging open startled everybody. "Walt!" someone hollered.

Shana and her uncle glanced at each other. "That sounds like Matt Lawler," Shana said as she jumped up.

Dropping his burger, Joe followed her from

the back room. A guy in dirty construction clothes stood in the doorway, his face ashen.

"Matt? What's wrong?" Shana asked.

"We just heard over the scanner that they found a bomb at the ski jump," Matt exclaimed. "And it's set to go off in fifteen minutes!"

Chapter
Nine

O NE OF THE WORKERS found a timed incendiary device located at the top of the tower," Weems was telling the security crew gathered at the ski jump. "It was hidden in a brown paper bag like it was someone's lunch. The bomb squad is dismantling it. Our job is to comb the rest of the area. Look for anything suspicious, especially something hooked up with wires or batteries."

"What if we find something?" Joe asked.

"Alert someone from the bomb squad." Glancing down at a sheet of paper, Weems called out the areas each person was supposed to check. Joe and Frank were assigned the first floor of the tower, where the dressing rooms and locker area would eventually be housed.

As they headed to the tower, Frank said, "Gee, Weems is giving us the biggest area to search. Do you think he trusts us?"

Joe snorted. "No way. I think he figures we're expendable."

"Great." Frank grimaced. "Well, let's show him we can do our job."

When they went inside the tower, the two Hardys took different directions. The walls had just been sheetrocked and several rooms partitioned off, but not much else had been done. There didn't seem to be many places to hide a bomb.

Joe slowly walked from room to room. When he rounded a corner and entered what looked like the future locker-room area, he stopped dead. A brown paper bag was sitting at the base of the far wall.

Cautiously, Joe backed out, his heart pounding. Bombs could be so sensitive that any sound or movement might set them off.

"Frank," he whispered when he spotted his brother. "Alert the bomb squad. I may have found another one."

Ten minutes later two officers clad in eighty-five-pound bomb suits approached the brown bag. They moved slowly, like men walking on the moon. Joe, Frank, and Weems stood in the background behind a heavy protective shield.

As the officers neared the bag, Joe held his

breath. Even though the suits protected the men, they could still be knocked fifty feet if the bomb exploded.

When they reached the bag, one of them carefully peeled back the top. Joe could see the officer's shoulders relax. Turning, the man waved at Weems, signaling that it was okay.

Joe, Frank, and Weems rushed up. The officer held open the bag. Weems pulled on a latex glove and stuck his hand into the bag. He pulled out a piece of paper. On it was a message spelled out in letters cut from a magazine:

This is just a warning. Unless construction is stopped, next time there will be a bomb.

Joe glanced at the bottom. The note was signed Tyler Conklin.

"Allison, you are brilliant," Nancy told her friend as they headed into the glass-and-chrome office building in downtown Salt Lake City.

Allison grinned at the compliment. George and Nancy had borrowed skirts and blouses from their friend so all three were dressed for success. "We were just lucky State Senator Pavin was hosting an open house at his office."

"Do you think he'll be here?" George asked in a hushed voice. They had entered the building's spacious foyer. A small crowd had arrived for the open house, and a man with a nametag clipped to his suit jacket was checking them out before they could enter Pavin's ground-floor office.

"Who cares," Nancy said. "I just want to snoop around."

Allison and George laughed. "I doubt you're going to find anything that will tie the senator to Tyler's disappearance," Allison said. "He covers his tracks too well. The newspapers never found any trace of his receiving illegal campaign funds—and I'm sure they tried."

George cocked her head. "You don't know Nancy. I've seen her find clues in a totally empty room."

"In this case, we need to find out why Tyler printed out that information on Pavin," Nancy reminded them as they stepped to the front of the line.

"Good day, ladies," the man at the door greeted them courteously. "Are you with an organization?"

"Yes," Allison said. "We're representatives of Peace on Earth."

The man smiled. Nancy noted the name on his badge: Rolf Goodwin. One of Pavin's staff, she figured.

"Ah, Peace on Earth. Mr. Pavin thinks highly of your group's goals to protect the environment. Please sign the guest list, then go right in. There are refreshments and literature on the tables. If you have any questions, please don't hesitate to ask any of the volunteers. Mr. Pavin will be with us shortly."

"Thank you." Nancy scrawled her name on the clipboard he held, then hurried into the small suite. She wanted to get into Pavin's personal office before the senator arrived.

She walked over to the table and picked up a cup of tea and a brochure. Several volunteers and staff stood around, talking with interested visitors. Nancy slipped off and strolled down a small hall. She found what she assumed had to be Pavin's office. It was the only one with a huge teak desk and a window overlooking the city street.

"George," Nancy whispered when she found her friends eating doughnuts and sipping tea back in the main area. "I found Pavin's office and I'm going in. You and Allison hang out in front of the door so no one sees me. If someone comes, say 'Pavin' really loudly."

George nodded. The three girls walked nonchalantly toward Pavin's office. George and Allison blocked the doorway while Nancy darted inside. As the two girls chatted and ate appetizers, Nancy scooted behind Pavin's desk.

Nancy hunted through each drawer, keeping an ear tuned to her friends' conversation. She found notes, memos, and folders filled with documents but nothing that suggested any illegal activities. She opened the bottom drawer and found a day planner from the previous year.

Reaching into her purse, Nancy pulled out the computer printout they'd found in Tyler's book. She scanned the entries on the printout and matched them with the same date on the day planner. Excitement built as she realized there was a connection. For each date on the printout, the same day on the planner had been marked with an asterisk and initials.

Nancy copied the initials next to the corresponding date on the printout. She was almost done when she heard George call, "Look! Senator *Pavin* has finally arrived."

Hastily, Nancy ripped a page from the day planner, then stuck the book back in the drawer and shut it. Then she hustled across the office to join Allison and George in the doorway.

A tall, handsome man with graying hair had entered the suite. Rolf Goodwin made sure no one crowded too close to the senator.

Suddenly Goodwin glanced over at Nancy and studied her with narrowed eyes. Had he seen her come out of Pavin's office?

Nancy directed her attention toward Pavin, as if spellbound by his presence. Smiling and shaking hands, the senator greeted his supporters.

For a second Nancy closed her eyes and listened to his voice. Yes, he was definitely the well-dressed guy in Tyler's apartment. That meant her hunch was right. Tyler had something Pavin wanted.

Motioning for Allison and George to follow, Nancy left Pavin's suite. As they passed through the crowd, she could feel Rolf Goodwin's eyes on her. A shiver ran up her spine.

"What's the hurry?" George asked, racing after Nancy. She was still holding her cup of tea. Allison was awkwardly putting on her coat as she followed Nancy from the building.

"I need a phone book," Nancy said when they'd reached the sidewalk. She glanced right and left and spied a pay phone halfway down the street.

Nancy set off down the busy sidewalk. Snow was falling, and a layer coated everything like white frosting. Cars whizzed past, sending slush flying.

"What did you find in his office?" Allison asked when they reached the phone.

"Initials." Nancy opened the Yellow Pages to the section on building contractors.

Then she pulled out the computer printout. "See?" She pointed to the initials she'd written by each entry. "If my hunch is right, the initials will match up with some big business, maybe a company involved with building the Sports Park."

"You're right!" George pointed to a listing in the Yellow Pages. "Johnson Construction matches with JC."

"And Custom Builders of Utah matches with

CBU written here, next to an entry for a hundred thousand dollars." Allison gasped. "Boy, if this is right, they gave Pavin a lot of money."

Nancy closed the phone book. "Let's head to your dorm suite and check all the listings thoroughly. There might be companies listed under engineering and excavating firms, too."

"*After* we get some lunch," George insisted. "That doughnut is rattling around in my stomach."

Nancy grinned. "You're beginning to sound like Bess."

"There's an Italian restaurant around the corner," Allison said.

"So, what do you think the initials and dates mean, Nancy?" George asked as they walked down the sidewalk, which bustled with workers out for lunch.

Nancy pulled her coat more tightly around her. The wind had picked up and the air was icy cold. "I think our hunch about illegal campaign contributions might be right. If the companies listed here gave Pavin money, he might have promised them favors in return."

Allison nodded. "Sounds right. And if Tyler found out, he could have blown the whole scheme." She stopped in the middle of the sidewalk and grabbed Nancy's wrist. "That's probably why he split—not because he was guilty of sending those letters but because Pavin was after him!"

Nancy shuddered, remembering the suspicious look Goodwin had given her. Pavin's aide looked capable of protecting his boss, no matter what. Then a terrible thought crossed her mind. What if Goodwin and Pavin had already eliminated the problem? What if Tyler Conklin was dead?

Nancy shook the thought from her mind. No, she wasn't even going to think such a horrible thing, and she definitely wasn't going to voice her worry to Allison.

After a delicious lunch, the girls went back to Allison's dorm. As they climbed the stairs to the suite, Nancy told Allison and George what they needed to do.

"We need to match every initial with a company," she instructed. "Then we need to find out what, if anything, that company has been hired to do."

"I bet your friends Frank and Joe could help us," Allison said. She fished in her purse and pulled out her key. "At least they'd be able to tell us which companies got a lucrative contract for work at the Sports Park."

"Good thinking," Nancy said. Grinning, Allison swung the door open. When Nancy stepped into the suite, her mouth fell. The place had been ransacked.

"What happened?" Allison moaned.

"Looks like you were robbed," George exclaimed.

Nancy surveyed Allison's ruined suite. Drawers and cupboards had been emptied, the stuffing ripped from pillows, chairs were tipped over.

"Worse than a robbery, George," Nancy said, a lump catching in her throat.

She remembered the way Rolf Goodwin's eyes had followed her as she left Pavin's suite. Had the aide recognized Allison as Tyler Conklin's girlfriend and found out where she lived? Did he suspect they had the printout?

"If Pavin is the one after Tyler, then he must know we're onto him," Nancy said, unable to keep the fear from creeping into her voice. "And now they're after us!"

Chapter

Ten

WELL, I'M NOT AFRAID of them!" Allison thundered as she barreled into her dorm suite. Grabbing chairs, she righted them; picking up pillows, she punched the stuffing back in. When she turned to face Nancy and George, she had tears pooled in her eyes.

Putting her hands over her face, she suddenly collapsed on the sofa. George rushed over to comfort her. "Hey, it'll be all right. We'll call the police. They'll find the creeps who did this."

"I bet it's Rolf Goodwin." Nancy closed and locked the door behind her, then went over to the phone. "It might have been him with Pavin in Tyler's apartment."

She dialed the police station and asked for

Detective Urich. "They're contacting him," she said when she hung up. "Maybe this time they'll listen when you tell them that Tyler couldn't have sent the letter, that someone else is involved."

"Maybe." Allison wiped her tears on her coat sleeve. After picking up the phone book, Nancy sat down to work. Before Urich arrived, she had to accomplish a lot.

Allison came over. "Let me help," she said, her voice clear. "I have another phone book in my room."

Nancy nodded, her mind already on the entries on the computer printout. If she was right, and someone knew they had the printout, she needed to figure out its importance—fast. Then she had to figure out who was after it, before she, Allison, and George found themselves in big danger.

Twenty minutes later Allison and Nancy had matched every initial with a possible company name. Detective Urich still hadn't shown up.

Nancy was tempted to call 911, which would dispatch a patrol car immediately, but then decided against it. She didn't want a couple of police officers stomping around the suite, asking a million questions and handling the case as if it were a simple robbery.

Nancy knew it wasn't a robbery because Allison had checked carefully—nothing had been taken. That meant the intruders had to have been looking for one thing—the printout.

"No wonder Pavin wants this," Nancy said, tapping the paper. "If this does indicate payoffs, your senator has been busy. According to this sheet at least ten companies gave him a total of a million dollars."

"And what did they get in return?" George asked.

Allison stretched her legs. She'd changed into jeans. Nancy was still in her skirt and blouse.

"Pavin could have promised them lots of things—like legislation favoring their businesses," Allison said. "And, of course, there's his well-known stand on the environment."

"Meaning?" Nancy asked.

"Meaning he tells whatever group he's speaking to what they want to hear. When he spoke to Peace on Earth, he had the nerve to brag about his pro-environment record." Allison snorted. "Which doesn't exist at all."

Just then the doorbell rang. Allison jerked upright, and even Nancy's heart skipped a beat. But then she quickly reassured herself that Pavin or his goon, Rolf Goodwin, would hardly announce themselves.

Still, she peered through the peephole. Detective Urich was holding his badge in front of it.

"Sorry I couldn't get here sooner," he said when Nancy opened the door. Stepping into the suite, he glanced around. "Housecleaning?" Immediately, he held up his hand in apology. "Sorry. It's been a long day. So what happened, and why didn't you call a patrol car? An officer could have filed a report and we could be hunting for a suspect."

Nancy closed the door. Crossing her arms, she faced Detective Urich. She wasn't sure how much to tell the investigator. Would he think their story was crazy?

"We think we know who did it," Nancy said.

"Good." He pulled a pad from his pocket and flipped it open. "I need an easy case to solve. What's the person's name?"

"Senator Alexander Pavin," Allison blurted.

For a second Urich stared at his pad. Then he flipped it closed and stuck it in his pocket. "Okay, I'm out of here."

Nancy straightened. "Aren't you even going to listen to us?"

He eyed her wearily. "Three girls who are friends with Tyler Conklin? I don't think so. I think you got me here on a wild-goose chase to keep me from finding your boyfriend."

Nancy shook her head. "That's not true. Look, we have proof that something strange is going on. Something Tyler may have uncovered on Pavin. That's why he disappeared—he's hiding from Pavin."

Urich rolled his eyes skyward. "Miss Drew. Obviously you haven't heard the latest news."

"What news?" Allison said as she and George hurried to Nancy's side.

"A bomb was found at the ski jump at the Sports Park earlier today. It wasn't armed, thank goodness. But a note was found threatening to blow the place up next time unless construction was stopped. The note was signed by Tyler Conklin."

Allison inhaled sharply. "No, no way. Someone forged his signature."

Detective Urich shook his head. "We had the signature on the first threatening letter—the one sent to American Progress—analyzed. It's your boyfriend's signature, all right."

Nancy pressed her lips together. If Urich was right, then Tyler *was* behind the threats. That blew her whole theory that Tyler was in hiding for fear Pavin was after him. Which meant Pavin wasn't after the printout, either. But then, who had ransacked the apartment? And why?

"I don't believe you," Allison declared. Only this time Nancy heard the doubt in her friend's voice. The evidence was definitely stacking up against Tyler. "Believe me," Urich stated. "Tyler Conklin and his crazy EAAC cronies are behind the sabotage on the Sports Park. Thanks to a tip from the security crew at the park, we raided their warehouse on Twelfth Street."

Nancy started. She hadn't realized Frank would follow up on their encounter with Robyn Bickmore. But she guessed he'd had no choice.

Urich ran his fingers through his hair. His eyes were bloodshot, as if he'd been up all night. "EAAC had a printing press on the third floor. And the handouts they were printing were hair-raising. They were advocating a day-long, violent attack on environmentally unfriendly businesses everywhere. Here, in Utah, the target was the Sports Park."

"But—but . . ." Allison stammered. Her gaze sought Nancy's, pleading for help.

"Detective Urich, I don't doubt what you've discovered, but we have a hunch that Pavin has been taking bribes in return for kickbacks or payoffs or something. And we think that Tyler found out, which meant the senator was after him."

Urich chuckled. "And what politician hasn't been bribed? Face it, Ms. Drew. Your friend Tyler's up to his neck in trouble. The best thing you can do is get him to turn himself in," he added sternly.

Nancy returned his direct gaze. "Only we don't know where he is."

"Fine," he said tersely. "If you want to file a report about the break-in, I'll send over a police officer."

"No," Allison said quickly. "That won't be necessary."

After Nancy had thanked Urich and closed the door behind him, she leaned tiredly against it. Allison was staring at her, distrust in her eyes.

"You believe him, don't you?" she accused. "Which means you don't believe me."

With a sigh, Nancy rubbed her forehead. "Allison, you have to admit—"

"No!" Allison cut Nancy off. "I'll never give up. And if you and George aren't with me, then you're not my friends anymore." And with those angry words, she stomped into her room and slammed the door.

"This place is awesome," Frank told Kip as he viewed the snow-capped mountains. It was the day before Thanksgiving, and Weems had given the Hardys time off. A skeleton crew was guarding the construction sites. For once, Frank was glad Weems hadn't chosen them for the duty.

Joe straightened. He'd been adjusting his ski boots. Beside him, Shana fitted her goggles over her eyes. Everybody was dressed in warm ski clothes for a day of adventure.

It was early, and the sun was just peeking over the mountain range. Frank had never seen anything so barren, wild, and majestic. Since Kip knew every inch of northern Utah, he'd driven Shana and the Hardys high into a pristine backcountry area. They'd left Shana's car at the bottom, parking it on a service road. It would take about four hours of extreme skiing to reach the car.

By the time they were done, Frank knew they would be windburned and exhausted. But the thrill of swooping down rugged slopes covered with fresh powder would be worth it.

"Here, zip these into an inside pocket," Kip said, handing them each a small electronic device.

"What are they?" Frank asked.

"Locator beacons," Kip explained. "In case you're buried in an avalanche."

"Avalanche?" Joe repeated, sounding a little worried.

Shana patted his shoulder. "Don't worry. The chances are small we'll get in trouble. Still, yesterday's new snow plus the warmer weather predicted for today make for prime avalanche conditions."

Frank shot Joe a nervous look but then reminded himself they were skiing with two pros. Kip pointed to a pack on his back. "I brought a whole survival kit along—protein bars, cell phone, matches—just in case."

"You never can tell when something might happen," Shana added. "Most of our friends are into skiing in remote areas. And lots of them have had some kind of accident."

"That's reassuring," Frank quipped. Lowering his goggles, he stuck his ski poles into the snow, ready to push off.

Kip led the way.

Thirty minutes later the foursome stopped on a ridge below two outcroppings of rock. Frank thought the view was breathtaking. The snow-topped pines silhouetted against the bright blue sky looked like the picture on a postcard.

"How about one of those protein bars?" Joe said, panting. He was stooped over, trying to catch his breath. "I'm bushed."

Lifting up her goggles, Shana laughed. "Hey, tough guy, we're only a third of the way to the bottom."

"This is a good place to rest, though." Kip pulled off his knapsack and sat in the snow, setting his poles against a conifer tree. "Some prime scenery."

"That's for sure." Frank pointed to the top of one of the rock formations. "I'm going up there to see if I can get a three-hundred-sixty-degree view."

Turning on his skis, he began to work his way up the slope. A gust of wind whipped over the edge, and he pulled his wool cap lower around his ears.

"Be careful," Kip called when Frank was about halfway up, then hollered something else Frank couldn't hear.

Sticking his poles in the snow, Frank made his way to the top of the rock. By the time he reached the pinnacle, his chest was heaving from the high altitude and the climb. But the effort was worth it. From his perch, he could see in all directions.

"Awesome!" he hollered down to the others. Shana waved. Joe held up a protein bar and rubbed his stomach.

Frank grinned. The view, the air, the day—it was so exhilarating, he felt as if he could ski Mt. Everest. Glancing down at his friends, he saw Kip gesturing for him to rejoin them.

Frank checked out the dish of snow between the two ridges. It was perfectly smooth, like a groomed ski slope. If he whizzed down it, he'd be back with his friends in an instant.

Bending, Frank took off as a low rumble from behind reached his ears. At the same time the snow underfoot abruptly gave way beneath him like a rolling wave of water.

The tips of Frank's skis dipped, then plowed into an upsurge of snow. With a cry, he somersaulted in the air. As he flipped, a wall of snow cascaded over him, pummeling him into the ground. Frank's head hit something hard, and all was dark.

Chapter

Eleven

"FRANK!" JOE SCREAMED. He started toward the rushing avalanche, but his brother had already disappeared in the mountain of snow. Frank would be buried alive!

"Stay back!" Kip hollered. Wrapping an arm around Joe's waist, Kip pulled Joe away from the edge of the avalanche fault while holding tightly to the trunk of a conifer with his other arm. Shana had skied to a grove of trees where she was safely out of the path of the avalanche.

"We've got to save him!" Joe struggled against Kip's hold. The roar of the avalanche was deafening, and the whole mountain seemed to tremble.

"We will," Kip shouted in his ear. "But we

can't be swept up in it, too. Try to keep your eye on the spot where you last saw Frank."

Joe nodded, understanding that they had to stay alive in order to save Frank. He grabbed the trunk and clung hard as the snow rumbled and broke like huge waves crashing on the shore. Then, suddenly, all was quiet.

Joe relaxed his grip. In shocked silence, he stared in front of him. The sun shone brightly on the new slope of snow as if the killing avalanche had never occurred. But there was no sign of Frank.

"It should be safe now," Kip said. He took off his pack and tied it to the branch of the tree. "We have to protect our emergency gear," he said, his movements quick and determined. "And no rushing off, Joe. I want you to follow my instructions. The new snow will be deep, powdery, and dangerous."

Joe swallowed hard. His first impulse had been to dash to the spot where Frank had disappeared, but Kip was right to warn him. If they were to find and save Frank, they would have to be careful.

After pulling the electronic beeper from his pocket, Kip turned it on. Just then Shana came up, her cheeks bright red. "Did you see where he went under?" she asked.

"Sort of." Kip handed her the cell phone. "Call the park service and tell them it's an emergency. Then help us search." Turning to Joe, he said, "Grab your poles. Then follow me—slowly."

The two set off in the general direction where they'd last seen Frank. Kip pointed to his left. "We need to criss-cross down the slope. Frank's got at least ten minutes of air. With the beeper, we'll find him before the time is up."

Joe nodded, but his heart was pounding frantically. What if they didn't find Frank before he ran out of air?

Kip socked him on the arm, trying to act casual to reassure him. "Come on."

The two worked their way across the unstable slope of snow, Kip listening for the beeper's signal. "This way," he called, as the beeper's tone grew louder. "Start poking around here. Slowly and gently. I'll work my way toward you from the other side."

Kneeling, Joe slid the four-foot pole into the loosely packed powder. Once, twice, three times it slid all the way to the end of the pole. Then, the fourth time, he hit something solid, but not rock-hard.

"Over here!" he shouted excitedly, then, bending, he called, "Frank!" into the snow beneath him.

Kip held the beeper directly over Joe's pole. It sounded wildly. "It's got to be him."

Dropping their poles, the two began to scoop

the snow away. Joe's heart raced as he shoveled handfuls to the side. By then Shana had joined them and was helping dig. All at once she gasped, "I feel something!"

She had uncovered a gloved hand.

"Frank!" Tears filled Joe's eyes. Working together, the three brushed snow from an arm, a shoulder, then a neck. Finally Frank's head and face were poking above the snow. His eyes were shut, but when Joe put his ear to his brother's mouth, he could feel the warmth of Frank's breath on his cheek.

"He's alive!" Minutes later they had Frank totally uncovered. His eyelids began to flutter.

"Don't move him," Joe cautioned. Kip might know about ski accident rescues, but Joe had trained to be a medic for another case. "We need to know for sure there are no injuries."

Just then Frank groaned and his eyes opened. Groggily, he stared at Joe, Shana, and Kip until his gaze cleared. His ski cap had been ripped off his head and his hair was covered with ice crystals. Struggling up on his elbows, he spit snow from his mouth.

"Wow," he finally gasped. "That was quite a rush!"

Joe let out a relieved guffaw. "Take it easy." He pushed him gently back in the snow. "You took a heck of a tumble."

"I'll get the thermos," Shana said.

With Kip's help, Joe checked Frank from head

to toe. When he'd decided there were no broken bones or head and neck injuries, he and Kip helped Frank escape from his snowy coffin.

Exhausted, Frank slumped beside Shana, who poured him a drink of steaming hot chocolate. "Umm," Frank hummed as he sipped. "This is great."

"You called the park service again?" Kip asked Shana.

She nodded. "I told them we'd found Frank. They were relieved. It seems the rescue team's on another emergency, so they might not get to us for a while."

"Tell them they don't need to come at all," Frank said. "I can make it down the mountain on my own." But when he tried to stand up, he fell back with a groan. "If I can borrow someone else's body. I think I'm bruised from head to toe."

"You'll also need to borrow someone else's skis," Joe reminded him. "They're buried under an avalanche of snow."

Frank suddenly looked grim. "Just like I was." He looked from Joe to Kip to Shana. "If it wasn't for you guys, I'd be a Popsicle by now."

A lump filled Joe's throat. If Kip hadn't equipped them with beepers, Frank might have been buried forever. "I bet you would have been all right," he said brightly. "It takes more than a few tons of snow to kill a Hardy."

* * *

"I know the day before Thanksgiving is a busy ski day," George said to Nancy, "but I didn't expect the slopes to be this packed!"

The two girls stood in the lift line at Snow Canyon Ski Resort. Nancy thought George sounded really disappointed. But then, she was disappointed, too. It was their first break since they'd arrived in Utah, and the lift lines were so long it would take them hours to get in one run.

Nancy sighed, thinking how much she needed a break. After Detective Urich's announcement about who had planted the bomb at the ski jump, Nancy realized that all her hunches had gone down the drain. And even though she and George had assured Allison they would continue to help find Tyler, their friend was still withdrawn.

"At least we got invited to a real Thanksgiving dinner tomorrow afternoon," Nancy said, trying to sound cheerful. "That was nice of Kip."

"Kip said his mom's holiday motto is 'The more the merrier.' Actually, we should have taken Kip and the Hardys up on their extreme-skiing offer," George grumbled. "By now we'd be whooshing down fresh powder."

Nancy punched her friend lightly on the arm. "*You* might be whooshing, but Allison isn't as good a skier as you are. I think the whole idea intimidated her."

"George! Nancy!" Allison's cheery voice made Nancy turn. Allison was coming toward them on her skis, a guy skiing next to her. He was stocky, with wavy blond hair. When he got closer, Nancy could read the insignia on his parka—"Snowy Canyon Ski Instructor."

"Meet James Kreiger, our savior," Allison said cheerfully. "James has offered to take us over to the back side of the hill. It's a lot less crowded."

"Great!" Nancy grinned.

James grinned back. He was in his mid-twenties, with an infectious smile and sparkling blue eyes. Nancy was immediately drawn to his boyish good looks.

"Allison assured me you were experts," James said. "Once we get up the lift, it'll be clear sailing."

"That sounds super to me!" George chimed in. "I wasn't too happy with the idea of skiing down a slope with a hundred other hotdoggers."

"I can understand that," James agreed, and he and George launched into a conversation about beginners getting on expert slopes before they were ready.

Seeing George's mood change, Nancy flashed Allison a grateful smile. Maybe the day was going to turn out okay after all.

But when she rode up the lift in the chair with Allison, her friend became somber. "I'm not as good a skier as you guys," she said, "but James assured me the back slope isn't too treacherous. Except for an occasional out-of-control snowboarder."

"You and I can always go down the regular run," Nancy suggested.

Allison shook her head firmly. "No. I want to make it up to you and George. I mean, you came all the way out here for a great vacation, and I've ruined it."

"No, you haven't." Nancy squeezed her friend's gloved fingers. "And don't worry about the slope. We can hang back and go a little slower." She nodded to the chair in front of them. George and James were still talking animatedly. "Let those two go ahead. They seem to have hit it off."

Allison grinned. "Yeah. James does seem like a nice guy."

Nancy's brows rose. "What do you mean he *seems* like a nice guy? Isn't he a friend of yours?"

"No. He came up and introduced himself. When I told him how disappointed we were that it was so crowded, he offered to take us down the back run."

Goose bumps prickled along Nancy's arms. Was James Kreiger who he said he was? But then she remembered the insignia on his jacket and his boyish smile, and she shrugged off her worry. Besides, she'd decided that Pavin wasn't after the printout. Two girls down the hall told Allison the suite had probably been trashed by pranksters from the guys' dorm.

As the lift carried them up the mountain, a brisk wind began to blow, rocking the chair.

Nancy glanced down at the skiers whizzing past on both sides. When they reached the top, she'd suggest they ski down one of the regular runs—just in case.

At the end of the lift, James and George slid from their chair and began skiing uphill toward a row of pines on the crest of the mountain. "Wait a minute!" Nancy called as she and Allison jumped from their chair.

George turned for a second, then kept going. Nancy glided after them, adjusting her poles as she went. Allison was right behind her. Cutting through the trees, James led them out of the shadows and into a sparkling expanse of white powder, marred only by a few track lines.

"Pristine, huh?" James grinned like an eager school kid showing off.

"Oh, it's perfect!" George gushed. "They don't have snow like this back East."

Nancy blew out her breath. It *was* gorgeous, and George was so excited she didn't have the heart to suggest the regular slope.

"Allison? Are you okay with this?" Nancy asked.

Her friend nodded. "Just no straight-down-the-hill for me, though. I'm going to stick closer to the left side, where it's not so steep."

"That suits me fine, too," Nancy said.

"Then let's go!" Putting on snow shades, James took off. George followed, whooping with glee.

Allison and Nancy pushed off at the same time. As she swooped through the soft powder, Nancy couldn't help but grin. It was so much fun!

Zipping left, then right, Nancy headed after James and George, but they quickly disappeared over a ridge. She glanced over her shoulder, catching sight of Allison, who had veered toward a grove of pines.

Nancy was turning left to get closer to Allison, when two skiers flew out from the pines. Wool ski masks hid their faces as they headed straight for Allison.

"Allison! Watch out!" Nancy screamed, but the wind tossed her words away.

Nancy raced toward her friend, hoping to warn her. She was too late.

One of the skiers had caught up to Allison and whipped in front of her. The other drew right alongside her. Nancy could see her friend twist her body and poles to the left in a desperate attempt to keep from crashing into them.

It was no use. The skier beside her swerved so close to Allison that he was able to reach out and snatch the cap off her head. Then the other crossed her path and clipped the end of her skis with his, forcing her into a fall.

Her legs and arms flying in all directions, Allison tumbled head over heels. Nancy sped toward her. To the left, there was a narrow ridge that rose into a peak, then dropped abruptly into a chasm below.

Nancy gasped. Allison was headed right for it! Out of control, her friend tumbled over the snowy ledge, disappearing from Nancy's sight.

"Help!" Nancy screamed. But the two masked skiers cut to the right in a flurry of flying snow and sailed over a bank in the opposite direction. Landing on the slope below, they skied out of sight.

Nancy zoomed to the edge of the chasm, plowing to a stop. Throwing up her sunglasses, she scanned the drop below. "Allison!" she screamed.

"Nancy!" The faint cry reached her ears. Dropping onto her knees, Nancy crept closer to the edge, dragging her skis beside her.

"Are you all right?" Nancy hollered. Inching forward, she caught a glimpse of her friend.

Allison was hanging against the side of an icy wall of rock, her legs dangling in the air. Nancy stifled a scream. Allison's grasp on a tiny, twisted juniper was the only thing keeping her from dropping to the rocks below.

Chapter
Twelve

"HANG ON," Nancy called, trying to remain calm even though her heart was pounding furiously. How was she going to save Allison? She was as close to the edge of the chasm as she could get, yet there was no way she could reach her friend. And any slight shift in her body position might send her plunging over the cliff, too.

"I've got to get help!" Nancy hollered. "Don't give up."

Nancy carefully inched her way backward until she was able to stand on solid ground. By now James and George would be at the bottom. When they saw Nancy and Allison weren't behind them, would they set out to find them?

Probably, but then Nancy remembered the long lift lines. It would be at least half an hour before they returned. She didn't think Allison could hold on that long.

That meant she had two choices—wait for other skiers, or ski down to get help.

Planting her poles in the snow, Nancy started the climb back up to the main part of the slope. When she rounded the grove of trees, she saw three skiers moving down the run toward her.

Frantically, she waved. "My friend needs help!"

Within seconds, the three had pulled up in front of Nancy. One of them raised his goggles, his eyes full of concern. "We saw what happened to your friend. Is she all right?"

Nancy shook her head, her breath coming in gasps. "No! She fell over the cliff. Fortunately, she caught hold of a tree. But we have to get the Ski Patrol up here."

"I'll call." The third skier whipped a cell phone from her jacket pocket while Nancy led the other two to the edge of the chasm.

"Those two guys in ski masks purposefully forced your friend off the mountain," the second guy said. "We need to report them."

"I agree," Nancy said. "Except everything happened in such a blur, I don't even remember what color jackets they wore."

When Nancy reached the chasm, she dropped on her hands and knees and crawled to the edge. "Allison. I've got help."

Allison glanced up, her face tear streaked. One ski had fallen off. Nancy could see it lying on the rocks below.

"I'm slipping!" she cried.

"If we form a chain we can reach her," one guy said. "At least then we can hold on to her until the patrol gets here."

The woman came over. "They're on their way."

Quickly the four unsnapped the bindings on their skis. Linking hands, they formed a human chain, Nancy at the end. She held tightly to the wrist of the last guy and gingerly sidestepped to the edge. Using him as a support, she climbed over the rim and onto a narrow ledge of rocks below. From there, she was able to reach Allison.

"I'm going to grab your wrist, Allison," she instructed in a calm voice. "But don't let go of the tree. It might be a while before more help gets here."

Allison nodded weakly. Stretching as far as she could, Nancy was able to encircle Allison's wrist with her hand. She wanted to continue speaking to her friend, but the strain of holding her took all her effort.

"Nancy," Allison whispered. "I'm losing feeling in my arm. I don't know if I can—"

Just then a sprinkling of snow showered over them. Nancy swiveled her head, trying to see what had dislodged it. Relief flooded through her when she saw a woman wearing a ski patrol parka.

"Give us thirty seconds to secure our ropes and we'll get her," the woman told Nancy.

Tears filled Nancy's eyes. "Just thirty seconds, Allison. I know you can do it."

Soon a guy was dropping over the side of the cliff in a harness. With a practiced maneuver, he swung next to Allison and grabbed her around the waist. Nancy felt the strain lighten on her arm as Allison dropped wearily into the guy's arms.

All Nancy's nervous energy drained from her body. After the three skiers had hauled her to the top of the cliff, she slid down into the snow. Slowly, the ski patrol pulled Allison and her rescuer to safety. The three patrol members quickly checked Allison for injuries. Then they loaded her on their Sno-Cat.

Standing on shaky legs, Nancy thanked the three skiers again. "I owe you a hot chocolate. And I'd really appreciate it if you tell the ski patrol about the masked skiers. Four witnesses are better than one."

After Nancy and the others told their stories, the woman on the patrol radioed the ski lodge. "They might be able to catch the two at the end of the slope," she said, adding, "Though by now, they could be sitting by the fire in the lodge, laughing about their dangerous prank."

Prank? Nancy doubted it. Now that she knew Allison was safe, she had time to think about the sequence of events.

The masked skiers had attacked Allison as if they knew she would be there and what she would be wearing. They'd shot from the trees like arrows after a target.

But why were they after Allison?

Nancy frowned, angry at herself. She knew who had sent the attackers. Her instincts had told her something was fishy about James Kreiger. If only she'd listened, none of this would have happened.

"You'd better ride down with us," the woman called to Nancy. They'd already loaded her skis. Picking up her poles, Nancy again thanked the three skiers, who then took off. She climbed into the Sno-Cat beside Allison, who was sipping something warm from a thermos. She gave Nancy a grateful but exhausted smile.

As the Sno-Cat rumbled toward the resort, Nancy became anxious about George. She honestly didn't think Kreiger would go after George, but until she saw her good friend, Nancy couldn't relax.

As the Sno-Cat slipped down the crowded slope, Nancy caught sight of George waiting in the lift line. Relief washed over her.

Scanning the line, she hunted for James. Just as she had expected, he wasn't there.

"Excuse me." She tapped the woman patrol member on the shoulder. "Does the resort have a ski instructor named James Kreiger?"

"Never heard of him," the woman replied.

"What happened?" George exclaimed when the Sno-Cat halted outside the patrol house.

Nancy climbed out. "It's a long story."

After the patrol had written up a report on the accident, Allison, Nancy, and George went into the lodge.

"Once again I ruined a nice day," Allison said ruefully as they settled into a comfortable sofa in front of a roaring fire. Nancy ordered hot chocolate for everyone. "It wasn't your fault, Allison. Those two skiers went after you."

"What are you talking about?" Allison looked surprised.

Nancy leaned closer. "I mean, they knew you were coming. They forced you off that cliff on purpose, which means somebody tipped them off that you were skiing down that back slope."

"What!" George and Allison cried in unison.

"George, where did James go after you two reached the lodge?" Nancy asked.

"He said he had a lesson to teach."

"The woman on the ski patrol said there was no instructor named James Kreiger."

Allison's mouth dropped open. "You mean he tipped off the guys who went after me?"

"That's crazy, Nancy," George protested. "When could he have contacted them?"

"It would take only a couple of seconds before you got on the lift if he had a cell phone or walkie-talkie."

"But why would anybody go after me?" Allison asked. "I figured the two had dared each other—you know, to steal my ski cap. They probably didn't even realize I had tumbled over the cliff."

Frowning, Nancy shook her head. "No. It was more ruthless than that. And I bet it has something to do with Tyler, Pavin, the printout, and your suite being trashed." With a frustrated sigh, she slumped back on the soft sofa cushions. "I just wish I could put it all together."

"It's going to get dark soon," Kip said as he looked west at the sun setting behind the Oquirrh Mountains. "I wonder what's keeping the park rangers."

The four were huddled in the shelter of the conifer trees, where the snow wasn't so deep. Kip had spread a reflective blanket on the ground for everybody to sit on, and they'd had an early dinner of dried fruit, hot chocolate, and power bars.

Still, Frank's stomach grumbled with hunger, his feet were getting cold in his ski boots, and every bone and muscle in his body ached. He was also cursing himself right and left. If it hadn't been for his stupidity they wouldn't be in this fix.

"They should be here by now," Shana said, checking her watch. "I'm going to call again."

Pulling out her cell phone, she dialed. After identifying herself, she again told the caller on the other end what the emergency was and where they were stranded. When she finished, she looked at Kip with a worried expression. "The ranger said they just had another emergency where there were bad injuries. We're low priority." Glancing at the darkening sky, she shivered.

Frank stood up, trying not to grimace at the pain in his muscles. "Then we have only one choice. We hike back to the car."

Kip snorted. "Are you nuts? There are drifts of snow three and four feet deep. Unless we all had snowshoes, we'd never make it back."

"Oh." Frank hadn't thought about that. "Then you three should ski down to Shana's car and get help."

This time Joe objected. "Kip and Shana can ski to the bottom before it's dark, but I won't leave you."

"But I—" Frank started to protest.

Kip raised one hand to silence him. "No use arguing. It's too dark for any of us to ski out. In this light, one of us would end up headfirst in a snowdrift or falling off a cliff."

125

Grinning, Shana settled closer to Joe. "So we'll just have to snuggle for warmth. And look on the bright side: We'll be back tomorrow in time for turkey dinner."

Joe grinned happily at Shana, so Frank knew his brother liked the idea of staying out for the night.

With a sigh, Frank sat back down. His head hurt and his neck was so sore he couldn't move it. In this condition, he probably wouldn't have made it up or down the mountain.

"We'll find a spot to build a snow shelter," Kip said. "And there's enough old wood here for a small fire."

"See?" Shana jumped up with a cheerful smile. "It'll be just like camping out."

While Joe, Shana, and Kip worked on constructing a snow cave against the face of a rock, Frank gathered wood. The dried limbs of the conifers were brittle and small, but he knew they'd catch fire quickly.

Soon pitch-black darkness descended on the camp they'd created. Frank laid a fire at the mouth of the almost-completed cave, which had two sides and a roof of snow to help keep out the bitter wind. When he lit the wood, a soft glow filled the site. Maybe a night in the wilderness wouldn't be so bad after all.

A low noise awoke Frank. He tried to remember where he was. He sat up and glanced around, wincing as his muscles protested his change in position. The dying embers of the fire reflected off the walls of the icy lean-to, and beyond that the snowy slope glowed blue from the light of the moon.

The noise came again, only this time Frank recognized it—the hum of a motor. Had the Park Service arrived to rescue them?

Pushing up the sleeve of his parka, he checked his watch. Three A.M. He couldn't imagine that the rangers had come this late at night.

Shifting carefully so he didn't wake Kip, who was plastered against him on one side, and Joe, who slept on the other, Frank slid from between them and then went out of the cave. A blast of cold air hit his face. Rifling in Kip's backpack, he found a flashlight, but the sound of voices kept him from turning it on. Someone was out there. But who? And what were they doing in the middle of a wilderness area in the dead of night?

For a second Frank thought about waking Joe. But when he glanced into the cave, he saw his brother sleeping peacefully. He knew all three were exhausted. No use waking them up for what might be a wild-goose chase.

Still, Frank didn't click on the flashlight as he sneaked away from the campsite. The moon illuminated the mountainside, but he didn't need moonlight to see what was happening. On the top of the slope, a Sno-Cat was parked, its headlights shining on two men digging.

Digging? Frank knocked himself on the side of the head. Had his fall addled his brains? He tried to determine if the men could see him or his makeshift campsite. But the conifers and wall of rock hid the fire and the wind blew the smoke in the opposite direction, which meant the men had no idea Frank and the others were down below.

Stealthily, Frank worked his way up the hill, trying to stay in the shadows of rocks and trees. As long as the men stayed in the beam of the headlights, they'd be blinded so they wouldn't see him.

When he was about thirty feet away, Frank crouched behind a boulder and listened. The men worked silently, then straightened.

"Let's finish this up," one of them said. "Not only is it cold as the devil, but we need to be back before daylight. Don't want anyone spotting us."

Frank cocked a brow. What could they be doing that needed to be kept secret?

Suddenly, from down the hill, Frank heard Joe holler. "Frank! Where are you?"

Quiet, Joe! Frank wanted to shout. Quickly, he glanced up at the men. He could tell from their postures that they'd heard Joe calling.

Abruptly, they hurried to the Sno-Cat, throwing their shovels into the cab. When they stepped away from the headlights, Frank had trouble telling what they were doing. But he could see one of the men reach in and pull out two objects from the vehicle. He passed one to his partner as they moved into the moonlight.

Frank inhaled sharply. Both men were holding rifles with telescopic sights, and both were aimed in Joe's direction!

Chapter

Thirteen

Joe, TELL HARRY and Mike to grab the rifles!"
Frank called down the hill as loudly as he could.
He knew Joe wouldn't know what he was talking
about, but he hoped the men on the ridge would
get the message.

Twisting, he looked back up the hill. Fortunately, the men *had* gotten the message. Frank
could see that they'd stashed their guns in the
Sno-Cat and were jumping in after them now.
The vehicle took off with a roar. Several minutes
later the fading rumble of the motor told Frank
they were gone.

"Frank?" Joe called urgently. Frank hightailed
it down the hill, slipping and skidding in the
snow, and met his brother halfway up. He could

see Kip and Shana standing by the grove of trees in the moonlight.

Reaching up, Joe felt Frank's forehead. "Are you hallucinating?" he asked. "Or just having a nightmare? I mean, who are Harry and Mike?"

"No one." He gestured for Shana and Kip to join them, then told everybody about the men on the ridge.

"What do you think they were digging for?" Shana asked.

"Let's find out." Frank turned and led the way up the snowy slope. By the time he'd hiked to the top, he was puffing hard.

Clicking on the flashlight, he shone it around the area. The Sno-Cat had made distinctive tracks. When he found the spot where the two had been digging, he stooped to get a closer look.

The men had shoveled through the snow to the frozen ground, then used something sharp to dig six inches into the ground. Frank frowned as he tried to figure out what they'd been doing.

"Look at this," Kip said. Frank stood up. Kip was pointing to a small metal box, half buried in the snow.

"What is it?" Frank asked.

As he picked up the box, Kip brushed off the snow, then lifted the lid. "It's a mineral-deposit kit to test soil and ore samples."

"That's weird. Isn't this a protected wilderness area?" Frank asked.

Kip nodded. "Protected and public. Which is why our two midnight diggers didn't want to be seen."

"Hey, guys!" Shana called. She and Joe were searching where the Sno-Cat had been parked. "Look what we found."

Frank and Kip hurried over. Shana was holding a plastic-coated ID badge. "One of them must have dropped this in his hurry to leave."

Joe tapped the badge. "It's a nametag identifying an engineer who works for American Progress. The guy's name is Will Sutton."

"American Progress?" Frank repeated. "Why are they on park land gathering soil samples?"

Kip showed Shana and Joe the mineral-deposit kit. "I know exactly what they're doing," Kip said angrily. "They're trying to pull another fast one."

"What do you mean, *another* fast one?" Frank asked.

"Horst Kreig, the owner of American Progress, has purchased vast pieces of government-owned wilderness in the past. Each time his company has discovered huge mineral deposits *after* the land was assessed as being practically worthless."

Joe whistled. "So you think Kreig checks for minerals before he buys it?"

"I'd bet money on it. The environmental groups have been suspicious, but they've never had proof." Kip held up the mineral-deposit kit. "This might be the proof they've been looking for." He frowned worriedly. "The problem is, Kreig has got to have someone on the inside helping him get these deals through. So we're going to have to be careful when we pass along this information."

"State Senator Pavin?" Frank suggested. "His name was on that ripped-up letter to Ellman. Maybe Pavin's got his fingers in more than one illegal pie."

"We should investigate the other deals Kreig has made," Joe suggested. "It might help us figure out who else could be involved."

"I can help you there," Shana said. "An old boyfriend of mine works for the Bureau of Land Management. He might be able to get us government records on deals American Progress has made with the State of Utah."

"An old boyfriend?" Joe queried.

Shana batted her eyelashes coyly. "I have dated some, you know."

"I'd like to meet him, Shana," Frank said seriously. "Not that I know what we're looking for exactly. But it sounds like it points to American Progress. We also need to meet with Mr. Will Sutton. I'm interested to see what he has to say when we return his badge." Then Frank added with a grin, "And of course, we'll mention how we left the mineral-deposit kit along with his name at Park Service headquarters."

Joe punched Frank lightly on the arm. "I like your sneaky plan, brother."

Frank grimaced and rubbed his arm. "Of course, we have to *get* to forest headquarters first," he reminded them.

"Piece of cake," Shana said. "By morning, either the rangers will be here, or two of us can ski out. I've got extra skis in my car that we can bring back to you, Frank."

Frank gave the three a pained smile. Already, his muscles were stiffening from the cold. He couldn't imagine skiing down the hill. "I can't wait."

"James Kreiger, James Kreiger," Nancy repeated to herself as she broke six eggs into a bowl. It was morning. The girls had gotten home from their ski adventure late the night before. All three had fallen into bed exhausted and slept until almost nine.

Now George was in the shower, and Allison was slumped on the sofa, sipping hot tea. Nancy had woke up refreshed, but her arm hurt. She could only imagine how stiff Allison was from hanging on to that juniper.

As Nancy whipped the eggs for omelettes, her mind whirled with thoughts about the near disaster on the mountain. Yesterday, before they left for home, she'd checked with the manager at Snow Canyon Ski Resort. No one by the name of James Kreiger was employed by them, the woman had told her. As soon as she got back to the dorm, she'd checked the phone book. No Kreigers at all.

Of course, the guy probably hadn't given them his real name. Still, Nancy was determined to figure out a connection, a clue, *something*.

"So, what time are we supposed to be at Kip's house?" Allison asked. "An old-fashioned turkey dinner sounds heavenly."

"Two this afternoon." Nancy poured the first omelette into the hot, buttered pan. "While we're there, I'd like to pick Frank and Joe's brains. Maybe they've come up with a lead on their case that might help us. After all . . ." She was about to say that the Hardys were also investigating Tyler but decided not to because she knew Allison would just get angry.

"Yeah, well, don't talk with them while I'm around," Allison grumbled. "Because if they mention anything about Tyler blowing up that ski jump, I might have to bean them with the turkey."

Nancy laughed. "Well, just don't bean them until I get a big slice of white meat."

Allison giggled, and Nancy was glad to see that her friend's sense of humor was returning.

"Boy, did that feel great!" George called from the hallway. She was wrapped in a towel, her hair damp and uncombed.

"First omelette's ready," Nancy sang out. The

table was set and Allison had made a fresh fruit cup. Nancy's stomach grumbled, but she didn't want to eat so much that she'd ruin her appetite for Thanksgiving dinner.

"Let's take it easy this morning," Allison suggested as she poured everyone orange juice. "I'll show you around campus."

Nancy placed the first omelette on the table. "Good idea."

It would give her time to think about what she wanted to ask Frank and Joe. If anybody could help her sort out her clues—and nonclues—it would be the Hardys. And maybe they had dug up evidence that would help her figure out who was after Allison, which might just give her an answer to the biggest mystery of all: Where was Tyler Conklin?

"And I thought *we* had an adventure yesterday," Allison said. "At least we didn't have to spend the night in the mountains and scare off gun-toting diggers."

Allison was sitting beside Nancy on the sofa in the Coleses' family room. George and Kip sat next to each other on the brick hearth, their backs to the crackling fire. Frank was perched beside Nancy on the arm of the sofa. Uncle Walt lounged in a recliner by the fire, and Shana and Joe were in the kitchen helping Mrs. Coles wash the Thanksgiving dinner dishes.

"Well, I'd say you had a hair-raising adventure, Allison," Frank said. "I only got blended by an avalanche, but you almost turned into scrambled eggs."

"Frank," Nancy protested.

Allison chuckled. "Actually, that's not all that happened . . ." she began, but Nancy shot her a warning look. She'd already warned Allison and George not to mention James Kreiger. She wanted to talk over her suspicions when she was alone with Frank.

"When did the park rangers show up with their rescue vehicle?" George asked Kip.

"Early this morning, thank goodness. Otherwise we would have had to execute Plan B."

"Plan B?" Allison repeated.

Frank chuckled. "That was the Torture Frank Plan. I would have had to ski down the mountain." He pushed up the sleeves of his sweater. His arms were dotted with bruises. "Who says snow is soft and fluffy?"

"Not me." Kip shook his head. "I've done bellyflops and dives into too many snowbanks."

"Who's up for dessert?" Shana called into the living room.

"I am," rang out a chorus of voices.

When Frank started to stand up, Nancy gestured for him to wait. He nodded and, when they were alone, sat down on the sofa beside her.

"What's up?" he asked.

"Plenty." She told him her theory about Allison's accident being no accident, and how she suspected James Kreiger was involved.

"Wow. That's heavy duty." Frank sat back. "But why would someone be after Allison? Does it have to do with Tyler?"

Just then George brought them each a slice of pumpkin pie heaped with whipped cream. Nancy gave her a grateful smile. When George left, she filled Frank in on the trashed dorm suite and the visit from Detective Urich.

"Urich was right about the bomb threat," Frank said. "Joe found the letter from Tyler. He threatened to blow up the ski jump if construction didn't stop." Slowly Frank ate a forkful of pie. Nancy watched while he chewed and swallowed, hoping he'd come up with some wonderful insight on what had happened to Allison.

"Well?" she prompted.

"Umm," he hummed, his eyes closed. "This is the most wonderful pie I've ever eaten."

"Frank, you say that every time you eat pie. I'm floundering with this case. Would you *please* help? Evidence keeps pointing to Tyler Conklin being this mad bomber, only my friend Allison insists he has to be innocent. Then I find out Tyler's got some secret on Senator Pavin, and I begin to wonder if Allison isn't right—"

Frank bolted upright. "Tyler has something on Pavin?"

"Yes." Nancy told him about the printout. "We think Pavin must have been getting campaign contributions from big companies for political favors. We went to Pavin's office, and I found dates on a calendar corresponding to dates on the printout." When Nancy finished talking, Frank set his plate on an end table, his pie only half eaten.

"Whoa. That's interesting." Tilting his head, Frank studied Nancy.

She narrowed her eyes. "If you know something, Frank Hardy, you'd better let me in on it," she warned.

"Okay. But remember, all we have are hunches." Frank told her about finding the ripped-up letter in Ellman's office.

"So Pavin must have promised Ellman a lucrative contract in return for—?" Nancy guessed.

"We don't know what Pavin was getting. But obviously, it didn't work out. Ellman didn't get the contract and consequently went bankrupt."

"But that's more proof that Pavin is dirty!" Nancy exclaimed. "Which means Tyler might have gotten something on him. Something so devastating to Pavin's career that he had Tyler . . ."

Her voice trailed off. Nancy turned wide eyes on Frank. "Whoever forced Allison off that cliff yesterday meant business. In fact, I think they were trying to kill her. What if . . ." She dropped her voice to a whisper so no one in the kitchen could hear. "What if Tyler Conklin is already dead!"

Chapter
Fourteen

I CAN'T IMAGINE Tyler's dead," Frank said as he picked up his plate. "Why would a senator kill some college kid just because he knows something about him?"

Nancy stabbed her fork into her pie. "It's no harder to believe than that an environmental group is bombing the Sports Park!" she countered. "And Tyler isn't just an ordinary college kid. He has pretty strong convictions."

"Which makes him sound even guiltier. Especially if he's linked to Earth at All Costs."

Nancy shot him an angry look. "You don't really believe Bickmore and her buddies from EAAC blew up the bobsled run?"

"Why not? I got a look at one of the flyers they were printing in that warehouse. It spouted some pretty radical stuff. Weems is working with the police on investigating them, so maybe they'll come up with something."

"They won't," Nancy declared. "Because then that would make Tyler guilty. And I'm beginning to side with Allison. Something else is going on here—something political that has to do with Pavin and large, influential companies like American Progress."

"American Progress?" Frank almost dropped his fork.

"Don't tell me you've uncovered something on them, too!" Nancy scooted closer, her eyes gleaming. She'd been right. Frank did know things—lots of things—that could help her investigation.

Frank told Nancy about the badge and mineral-deposit kit. "Kip's hunch is that Horst Kreig, the president of American Progress, is illegally checking for minerals on state land. If he finds anything that looks promising, he sets up a deal to buy or swap the land—for almost nothing."

"Horst *Kreig?*" The name jolted Nancy. "That sounds a lot like the name Kreiger."

Frank frowned uncertainly. "Come on, Nan. You're not saying someone from American Progress went after Allison."

Nancy forced down her last bite of pie. All at once it didn't taste so delicious. "What if

Pavin and American Progress are in this together?"

"That has crossed my mind. Kreig has to have someone on the inside to make these deals go through the state legislature so easily. And Pavin could be the one."

Nancy slumped back. For a second she and Frank just stared at each other.

"So, how do we get to the bottom of all this?" Nancy asked.

"We have a name from that badge," Frank said. "Tomorrow, while Joe and Shana are talking to Shana's friend at the Bureau of Land Management, I'm paying a surprise visit to Will Sutton at American Progress."

"I want to be there," Nancy insisted. "Maybe I'll bump into someone named James Kreiger. If I do, I plan on finding a tall building to push him off."

"What are you hoping to find?" Shana's old boyfriend, Kenneth, asked as he led Joe and Shana down the hall of the deserted building. Since it was the day after Thanksgiving, the government offices were closed. Shana had had to sweet-talk Kenneth into meeting them downtown on his day off.

Joe studied the tall, handsome, preppie-type guy wearing chinos and loafers. Probably graduated with a degree in business, Joe thought grumpily. What had Shana seen in a guy like that?

Trying not to appear too jealous, Joe watched Shana flirt with Kenneth as they walked ahead of him down the hall. She'd worn a clingy dress in some kind of soft fabric and fashionable boots. It was the first time he'd seen her in something other than coveralls or snow gear. She looked great, and her walk was so—so feminine.

"We're hoping to see records of land purchases made by American Progress or Progress Development," Shana said. Glancing over her shoulder, she smiled at Joe. "Right?"

"Uh, right," Joe stammered. He'd been concentrating on Shana so hard, he'd forgotten Kenneth's question for a second. "Plus we'd like a printout of all the mines American Progress owns in the state."

"And what is this for, Shana?" Kenneth asked, sounding slightly suspicious.

Shana linked her arm with his and whispered. "I know Joe looks like a high-school kid, but he's really a private detective working undercover with the Building and Games security crew on the sabotage at the Sports Park."

High-school kid! Joe fumed. Biting back a grin, Shana winked at him.

Kenneth stopped in front of a locked office door. Turning, he gazed at Joe with interest. "No kidding?"

"No kidding." Joe crossed his arms and scowled seriously, trying to look like a private detective.

"What do mines and land deals have to do with the Sports Park?" Kenneth asked.

Joe arched one brow. "That's what we'd like to find out," he said mysteriously.

"Oh." Kenneth unlocked the door, then led them to a small cubicle, where he turned on his computer. "While it warms up, I'll get you a copy of any studies or data we might have in the files. The bureau's got tables and charts on everything."

"That'd be great!" Shana gave him a warm smile. When he left, Joe slipped his hands around her waist and pulled her close against his chest.

"You don't have to be quite that nice to him," he whispered in her ear, her hair tickling his nose.

She giggled. "I thought that was how spies acted. You know, disarm the unsuspecting person with your charm."

"Oh, no. Usually they wear false mustaches and baggy pants and growl a lot." He nibbled on her neck and was about to kiss her when Kenneth came back.

The two of them sprang apart. "The computer's booted up," Joe said quickly.

Kenneth handed him several pieces of paper,

then sat down at his desk. "Okay. Let's find the file on American Progress or Progress Development." After lots of key punching and mouse clicking, Kenneth gave a satisfied, "Ahhh."

Minutes later the printer spewed out several sheets. When it was finished, Kenneth ripped them off.

"Here's a list of all American Progress land holdings, as well as a list of the company's mines."

Joe scanned it quickly. A grin spread across his face. "This is great. It's got everything we need—original purchase price, current values, what the land is being used for, mining rights." He slapped Kenneth on the shoulder. "Thanks."

"No problem." Kenneth smiled at Shana. "Shana, you owe me one."

"I'll send you courtside tickets to a Utah Jazz basketball game," Joe said. Without waiting for a reply, he grabbed Shana's hand and pulled her from the cubicle.

"How are you going to get courtside tickets?" Shana asked as she hurried down the dark hall after him. "They're impossible to get."

Joe grinned. "I'm not. I just didn't want you owing him one."

When they left the office building, Joe blinked in the winter sun. It was almost lunchtime. They weren't supposed to rendezvous with Frank until afternoon.

"How about if I take you out for lunch?" Shana suggested as they headed for her pickup truck. "Cole Construction" was printed on the side. The vehicle was covered with mud from building sites, and an array of tools and supplies filled the truck bed.

"Sounds good to me." Opening the door, Joe stood back, bowing like a chauffeur. "Madame, your chariot awaits."

"Thank you, kind sir." Shana climbed into the high cab of the truck as gracefully as she could. When Joe jumped in the passenger seat, she peeled away from the parking lot.

"I know a wonderful inn. They have a lunch buffet, roaring fire, and a view of the city."

"Sounds great," Joe agreed. Half an hour later they had left the city and were winding into the mountains. As Shana drove, Joe scanned the computer printouts.

"It looks like we were right," he said. "Kreig and two of his companies, American Progress and Progress Development, have made fortunes off the land they've bought from the government. They buy it cheap, then either develop it or mine it."

"That's what they're trying to do in Park City, too," Shana said. "Kreig wants to turn this beautiful wilderness area into a resort. He keeps saying how much it will benefit the community." She gave a snort of disbelief. "But it sounds to me like the resort is going to cater to wealthy retirees or out-of-town skiers. We hard-working Utahans probably won't be allowed to set foot on their exclusive ski slopes and golf courses."

"Then why do all these deals go through?" Joe asked.

"Connections. Kreig's got lots of politicians in his hip pocket. He's rich and influential. Plus he does pay lots of taxes and employs many people. Even my dad's working for him, in a way, since American Progress is the overall contractor for the Sports Park."

After rolling up the papers, Joe tapped them on his knee. "Proving Kreig did anything illegal will be difficult."

Shana nodded. "He seems to keep his nose clean." She swung the pickup around a switchback. Joe grabbed the dashboard. "Whoa. That was a sharp one."

"Seasick?" She laughed.

Joe glanced out his window. Beyond the guardrail, the mountainside fell sharply into a snow-covered valley. Since there were no leaves on the trees, he could see for miles.

Frowning, Shana looked in her rearview mirror. "That Bronco is sure hugging my tail. Makes me uncomfortable."

Joe twisted to look out the back window. A gray vehicle was right on their bumper. He could just make out two men in the front seat. "Maybe they don't want to miss the buffet."

Just then the Bronco sped up, darted into the left-hand lane, and pulled up beside the pickup.

"That's crazy," Shana declared. "He's going to get us both killed."

Leaning forward, Joe peered around Shana. The guy in the passenger seat was rolling down his window. Joe was about to yell for him to get out of the lane, when the guy stuck a gun barrel out the open window.

"Shana!" Joe hollered. "He's got a gun!"

With a scream, Shana whipped the steering wheel to the right. Joe was thrown left, then bounced in the air as the pickup hit the gravelly shoulder.

Reaching over, he grabbed the steering wheel to steady the pickup before it scraped the guardrail. "Easy!"

"Oh my gosh!" Shana took a deep breath. "That scared me to death."

"That makes two of us." Joe whirled in his seat. The Bronco had fallen behind them, but he knew it wouldn't be long before the gunman pulled up and tried for another shot.

"How far to the inn?" Joe asked. He had no idea who the two creeps were, but it was obvious they were serious.

"Too far. And there isn't even a gas station or a turnoff." Shana's eyes darted to the rearview mirror.

"We've got to do something. They're going to try it again."

"Joe, do you trust me?" she asked quickly.

"Trust you?"

She nodded. "There's a granddaddy of a hairpin turn up ahead. There's also a runaway-truck ramp cut in the embankment on the other side. You know, one of those turnoffs for drivers to use if their brakes fail as they're going down the mountain."

"Yeah." Joe got the picture. Sort of.

"I need you to keep your eye on the Bronco," Shana instructed. "Tell me when it's almost beside us and accelerating."

"Got it." Joe made sure his seat belt was fastened, then turned so he could watch the Bronco.

Shana stepped on the gas and zoomed around the next curve. A road sign warned drivers of the upcoming hairpin turn. Joe hoped the two goons in the Bronco wouldn't see it.

"Here they come," he said. "And they're traveling fast."

Shana took a deep breath. Joe gripped the door handle. His gaze snapped from the Bronco to the road. As Shana rounded the bend, he watched the sharply curved guardrail.

"Ready?" Shana asked.

Out of the corner of his eye, Joe saw the gun poke out of the window. "Go!"

Shana slammed on the brakes. At the same time she cut the steering wheel hard to the left and accelerated into the runaway-truck ramp.

The truck hit the soft road with a seat-jarring jolt, then lurched to a stop. Whipping around, Joe looked behind him as the Bronco, which had been speeding up to catch them, zoomed straight for the guardrail. With an ear-splitting crash, it broke through, flew for an instant, then dropped out of sight.

Chapter

Fifteen

JOE RACED from the pickup truck and across the road, Shana on his heels. When they reached the smashed guardrail, they slid to a stop and peered down the embankment.

The Bronco had landed about fifty yards down the slope, its flight cut off by a stand of trees. The front end was completely smashed, the hood crumpled against the windshield. Joe doubted that anyone could have survived the impact.

"Stay here and flag someone down," Joe told Shana. "Have them call nine one one. I'm going down there."

Leaping over what was left of the guardrail, Joe half-slid, half-stumbled to the Bronco. The vehicle had hit the ground with such force that the tires had blown and the roof had caved in.

Bending, Joe stared into the front seat, gulping at the grizzly scene. Neither of the men had been wearing seat belts and consequently were thrown around.

Who were they? Joe wondered. And why were they shooting at him and Shana?

The window was still down on the passenger side. Carefully Joe reached in, feeling for the man's pulse. There was none. He could see the shooter's gun, lying on the floor of the Bronco. At least it was proof that they'd been fired at.

Joe made his way to the driver's side. He tried the door, but it was so crushed he couldn't get it open. Hastily, he went back around to the passenger side. If he reached in behind the first guy who was slumped against the dash, he might be able to grasp the wrist of the driver.

Trying not to touch the first man, Joe found the other's wrist. No sign of life. As he retreated from the car, his hand brushed against the passenger's back pocket. The top of a leather wallet stuck up.

Joe pulled out the wallet and opened it. Inside one of the plastic sleeves was an American Progress ID badge, just like the one they'd found in the national forest. Only this guy's name was Olchowski.

Joe glanced through the rest of the wallet. No family photos, no credit cards. Just a license confirming the name.

Joe put the wallet back, then wormed his way

out from the vehicle window. Hurrying back around to the driver, he studied the guy's bloodied face through the glass windshield. With a start, he realized he'd seen him before—he was one of Horst Kreig's bodyguards. When Joe straightened, his mind was racing. Why were two goons from American Progress trying to snuff them out? Heart thumping, Joe thought about Frank and Nancy, who were paying a visit to Will Sutton at American Progress. They could be in big trouble.

"I believe this is yours, sir," Frank said, watching Mr. Will Sutton's face when he held out the ID badge. He and Nancy were in a small office on the top floor of the American Progress building.

The entrance and reception area of the ten-story building was all polished mahogany, gleaming chrome, silk flower arrangements, and expensive artwork. In contrast, Sutton's cramped office was in an out-of-the-way back section with only one harried secretary for what looked like many employees.

"You found my badge?" A tiny vein began to throb in Mr. Sutton's temple, but he never lost his smile. "Why, I was wondering where it was," he said, his voice calm and controlled. "My family went cross-country skiing over the holidays. I must have dropped it."

Out of the corner of his eye, Frank could see Nancy's expression change. Her eyes narrowed and her mouth tensed when she heard Mr. Sutton's obvious lie.

Still smiling, Mr. Sutton took the badge. "Thank you, young man. Frank Hardy, you said?"

"Yes, sir. I work for the Building and Games security crew. That's how I knew about American Progress."

"Ahhh." Sutton nodded. "Well, thank you again." Walking over to the office door, he held it open. "Bad scene over at the construction sites. Are you guys close to catching the nut responsible for the bombings?"

"We're working on it." Without moving, Frank stuck his hands in his jacket pockets.

"Uh, thank you again," Mr. Sutton said, and when Frank didn't move, he asked, "Is there anything else?"

"As a matter of fact, we did find something else—right beside the badge. A mineral-deposit test kit. We left it with the park rangers."

He paused to let the information sink in. Sutton didn't even blink.

"Well, that's interesting." The man's voice was noncommittal. "Thank you for letting me know."

"You're welcome, and it was nice meeting you." On his way out, Frank shook Sutton's hand. As she left, Nancy gave him a friendly grin and a handshake, too.

"Say hi to James for me," she said cheerfully.

"James Kreig?" Sutton asked.

"Right."

"How do you know him?"

"Old high-school chums," Nancy fibbed smoothly.

Frank shook his head in amazement. Nancy had such a poker face, she could fool anyone.

When they reached the elevator and stepped inside, Nancy squeezed Frank's arm. "Did you hear that?" she whispered hoarsely. "James *Kreig*. Do you think Horst sends his son to do all his dirty work?"

Frank shrugged. "Before now, I didn't even know he had a son. I guess it could be good training for becoming the scheming, ruthless president of a big company."

"But why would someone from American Progress go after Allison?" Nancy asked. "The printout we found at Tyler's apartment wouldn't be that damaging to a corporation like American Progress."

"Unless Senator Pavin and Horst Kreig have other scams brewing," Frank guessed. "Maybe they're afraid if the police or some commission looks into campaign contributions, they'll uncover all sorts of schemes—like that land-swap deal Kip told us about in Park City."

Nancy nodded slowly, and Frank could tell she was deep in thought. "Only I think something else is going on," she finally said. "Something even more sinister. And it has to do with Tyler."

"What?"

The elevator stopped and the doors whooshed open. Linking her arm in Frank's, Nancy led him into the spacious foyer. "I wish I knew. Maybe Allison and George will uncover something. They're making the rounds of Tyler's friends, trying to find something that would lead us to him—or at least point us to the truth."

"Good plan. If we all work on this together, we may be able to crack our cases yet." As he pushed through the big glass doors, Frank let out an exasperated sigh. "Though our conversation with Sutton was a bust. He was tighter than a clam."

Nancy stopped to button her jacket. The sun was bright, but a cold wind funneled down the busy city street. "Not a total bust. You found out that whatever he was doing that night in the wilderness area was illegal, or at least sneaky. Otherwise, why would he have lied?"

"True. And he sure could lie with a straight face. Horst Kreig must have all his employees practice cunning and deceit. How many employees do you think Kreig has?"

Nancy glanced up at the tall office building that rose into the cloudless sky. "Hundreds," she guessed. "And that's just here in his administrative offices. He must employ thousands in his construction business, mines, engineering firms—you name it."

Frank whistled. "Which means that if he is

making crooked deals, he could be affecting and impacting on businesses, politicians, government employees, and civilians all over Utah."

Frank steered Nancy into the parking garage. They'd parked the Jeep on the lower tier. When they reached the elevator, Nancy punched the button for the lower floor, then grinned nervously. "You don't think this one's booby-trapped, do you?"

The elevator doors opened. Frank hesitated, remembering that night in the warehouse, then grabbed Nancy's hand and pulled her to the stairs. "I doubt it, but let's not take a chance."

When they reached Kip's Jeep, Frank checked his watch. "We're supposed to meet Shana and Joe back at Cole Construction in an hour. How about if we grab a bite to eat first?"

Nancy's stomach grumbled. "Good idea. I'm starved. I thought Sutton's secretary was never going to let us in to see him."

Unlocking the door, Frank climbed into the vehicle. When Nancy slid in, she turned to him with a worried expression. "You know, before we went in to see Sutton, the secretary had a few urgent conversations over the phone, then left the office for a while. You don't think . . . ?"

"They knew why we were there?" Frank finished. He thought a minute, trying to figure out why Sutton or anyone else in American Progress would be suspicious of a security guard with Building and Games. His boss, Roger Weems, worked closely with Horst Kreig and his men, so Sutton shouldn't have suspected anything.

"I don't know, Nancy. I can't imagine American Progress has anything to do with the sabotage of the Sports Park. Kreig and his company stand to lose millions if Utah doesn't host the Winter Games at the park or if the Olympic Committee chooses another site."

"It is confusing." Nancy hugged her jacket tighter around her chest. "Let's get out of this parking garage. It's like a dungeon in here."

Frank started the Jeep. "Tomorrow Kreig is dedicating the bobsled run. That's why Kip's uncle Walt and his crew are working so feverishly to finish it. Weems has all of the guards working tomorrow to make sure nothing goes wrong. He's still determined to pin the sabotage on Tyler Conklin and his cohorts at EAAC."

"And what about you? Are you still so sure?" Nancy looked at him directly.

Frank shook his head. "Not after all that's happened. Obviously, something fishy is going on with American Progress. But I think it's so big we may never get to the bottom of it."

Nancy gave him a confident grin. "Never say 'never,' Hardy." Her blue eyes twinkled mischievously.

Frank groaned. He'd seen that look many times. "What are you planning now, Drew? Breaking into American Progress—the most heavily guarded office building in Utah?"

"What a great idea!" Nancy laughed. "Why didn't I think of it?"

Pulling away from the parking spot, Frank headed up the one-way exit ramp that snaked through the garage. Suddenly he heard the roar of a motor and the squeal of brakes. An instant later a huge American luxury car zoomed around the corner. It was speeding the wrong way down the ramp, aimed straight at them.

"Frank!" Nancy screamed. "That car's going to crash right into us!"

Chapter

Sixteen

FRANK STOMPED hard on the brake, and the Jeep skidded to a halt. "Bail out, Nancy!" he hollered.

He heard the door open and caught a glimpse of Nancy rolling from the vehicle. With mounting horror, he watched the oncoming car bear down on him. Why, Frank wondered, would anyone try to ram one car with another? The other occupants would get as injured as Frank and Nancy. He had no time to dwell on this because he was too busy jerking the Jeep into reverse and flooring it. Fishtailing wildly, the Jeep flew backward down the ramp, the passenger door flapping.

As he looked over his shoulder, sweat popped out on Frank's forehead. Even though he was almost to the parking tier, there was no way he was going to get out of the way in time.

Then, out of the corner of his eye, he glimpsed two parking spaces. He backed into them and, without turning off the motor, opened his door and dove from the Jeep.

Ducking between parked cars, he ran toward the elevator. He heard someone yell and knew that whoever was in the attack car had gotten out. Then, a deafening *rap, rap* told Frank the person was shooting a gun.

Frank's heart raced. Had Nancy gotten away? Crouching behind a small compact, he stopped to catch his breath, then peered around the fender toward the stairs and elevator. There was no cover. He'd be a perfect target making his way for the exit.

"Frank!" When he whirled and saw that Nancy was hiding in the row across from him, he slumped forward in relief. At least she was okay—for now. But how were they going to get away without getting shot?

A movement made him scoot farther around the car. Two men walked slowly down the access aisle. Both wore dark suits and ties and looked like businessmen on steroids.

"Come on out, kids," one of them said. "We don't want to hurt you. We just have a few questions to ask."

Sure, Frank thought. Questions like, Where would you like to be buried?

If he and Nancy could elude the men, someone was bound to show up. Or maybe the parking attendant had heard the gunshots.

"Give it up, kids," the other guy said impatiently.

Frank hunkered lower, willing the men to walk by. Ages seemed to pass, and he thought they'd given up. But then he heard the soft tread of a footstep behind him, and before he could spin around, a cold, hard gun barrel was pressed into his neck.

"Give it up, girlie! We've got your friend!"

Nancy's heart fell. They had Frank!

"Come out or we'll shoot him." The man's voice came from her right.

Frantically, Nancy searched for something she could use a weapon. There was no way she was giving up. If she did, the thugs would shoot them both.

Her gaze landed on a piece of metal under the car beside her. When she peered closer, she could tell it was the handle of a jack someone had discarded.

Duckwalking silently, she made her way to the fender of the other car. She reached under it blindly, feeling around until her fingertips brushed the cold metal. Closing her fist around the handle, she drew it from under the car and cradled it to her chest.

Now she just had to find the right opportunity.

Minutes later she had her chance. The two guys were approaching the car she was hiding behind. They walked side by side, Frank in front of them. The goons were glancing right and left, and Nancy could tell by their relaxed postures that they weren't worried about some scared-to-death "girlie." One guy had even holstered his gun.

As they passed her car, Nancy waited until both of them glanced the other way, then waved, catching Frank's eye. He winked. Good, he knew she was there. As the trio moved up the aisle, she cautiously crept around the far side toward the hood of the car, careful to stay out of sight.

Then she sprang. Arm raised, she hit the thug holding the gun with all her might. He staggered, and the gun flew from his hand. Before the second guy could reach for his gun, Frank was on top of him.

Nancy pounced on the dropped gun, which was skittering across the concrete. Her hand closed around it just as the goon grabbed for her, knocking the jack handle from her grasp. Blood streamed down the side of his neck and his eyes were glazed over, but still he fought with her for the weapon.

Nancy yelled and kicked out at him. But he was twice as big and very muscular. He chopped at her wrist, trying to get her to release the gun.

Tears stung her eyes, but she held on. Then the

wail of a police siren reached her ears, and the thug sprang to his feet, yelling as he took off, "Let's get out of here!"

Frank still had the second guy pinned. Jumping up, Nancy aimed the gun at the struggling man. "Don't move," she warned. Behind her, she could hear sirens ringing and tires screeching. Then several uniformed officers raced into view and, kneeling, grabbed the guy Frank had been holding.

With a huge sigh, Nancy lowered the barrel.

"I'll take that." Someone carefully closed his fingers around hers and took the weapon. It was Detective Urich.

"What are you doing here?" Nancy asked.

"Saving you and your friend."

"But how did you know we needed help?"

"There was an accident up on the mountain. A guy named Joe Hardy—"

"My brother!" Frank cut into the conversation, frantic.

"He's fine. But the two maniacs who went after him and his friend, Shana Coles, are dead. Their car went over a ridge. When the responding officer stopped at the scene of the accident, Joe told him he'd checked the ID on the guys. Seems they were both employees of American Progress. He was really worried since you two were meeting someone at American Progress. The officer called it in. At first we were skeptical, but then someone reported hearing what sounded like gunshots in this garage. Luckily, there was a unit nearby."

"But what are *you* doing here?" Nancy asked.

Urich chuckled. "I was having lunch down the street. When I heard that two teens were in trouble, one named Nancy Drew, I figured I'd better investigate."

"Well, thanks for being here." A shout made Nancy turn. Two officers came up just then with the guy Nancy had whacked. He was handcuffed and held between the two men. Reddish brown blood was crusted on the side of his head.

"Read them their rights and take them in," Urich said. "They've got some explaining to do. We need statements from you two, as well," he told Frank and Nancy. "Your brother and his friend are already at the station."

Nancy nodded. Hunger and exhaustion made her legs wobbly. Reaching out, Frank took her elbow and steadied her. "Hey, thanks for saving my life," he said.

"Oh, you would have done the same for me, Frank Hardy." Nancy grinned at him. "Do you think those two will tell the police why they were after us?"

Frank squeezed her hand. "Let's hope. But I have a feeling they're going to demand lawyers, and American Progress should be able to afford the best. Besides, hired thugs don't usually spill the beans."

Slowly they made their way over to Kip's Jeep. Nancy was relieved to see that it wasn't damaged. After she got inside, she slumped back tiredly against the seat.

"Let's hope Detective Urich will take my suggestion seriously now—that there must be something big going on involving Pavin and American Progress," Nancy said.

"He can hardly ignore the printout you found in Tyler's apartment, after we show him the torn letter from Todd Ellman implicating Pavin," Frank said. "Then there's the mineral-deposit kit and the badge. It may not be enough to arrest Kreig or Pavin, but it may be enough to get the police department serious about investigating them."

"Good." Nancy sat up. "Because there are still too many unanswered questions. Like, Who's planting those bombs, who knocked Allison off the cliff, and where is Tyler Conklin?"

"The police are arresting Kreig right after the dedication of the bobsled run?" George hollered over the roar of the blow-dryer. "That's pretty dramatic."

"They want newspaper reporters from all over to cover the story," Nancy explained as she pulled on her boots. It was late the next morning, and the girls were headed to the dedication. "That way, even if Kreig's lawyers whisk him right out of jail, at least the media will know he's been charged with several counts of fraud *plus* conspiracy to commit murder."

Allison pulled her wool sweater on over her head. "So those goons who attacked you spilled the beans?"

Nancy nodded. "They said Kreig instructed them to 'silence' us. Pavin must have told him."

"That makes sense, but how did Kreig know about Joe? He was attacked before you and Frank even went to American Progress to confront Sutton."

"Frank thinks they identified Joe with the telescopic sights on their rifles the night Frank and Joe were trapped on the mountain. It's the only explanation," Nancy answered her friend.

Choosing a warm wool cardigan, Nancy slipped it on over her turtleneck. Since they'd be outside all day, the girls were dressing for extreme cold. "The goons didn't talk until Will Sutton turned himself in—voluntarily—and told the police all he knew."

"Sutton had an attack of the guilts, and he confirmed the Hardys' hunch about the company illegally checking for minerals before purchasing what was considered worthless land."

"And Pavin's part in it all?" Allison asked.

"The police are working on it. But it's pretty clear Pavin was necessary to get the shady deals through the legislature—for a big, illegal payoff, of course."

"So everything's falling into place, right?"

Turning her head this way and that, George checked her hair in the mirror. Nancy grinned, knowing her friend was eager to see Kip.

Suddenly Nancy heard a sob. Allison plopped down on the bed, crying. "Wrong. Why haven't we heard anything about Tyler? Why aren't the police listening to us about him? Don't they see that if Pavin is mixed up in this, it means he had a reason to discredit Tyler? He made it look like Tyler was sending those threatening letters."

Her last words grew garbled as she burst into sobs. Nancy and George sat down next to her.

"Detective Urich *is* listening," Nancy said, trying to soothe her friend. But her heart was heavy. The police *had* been listening—listening to Robyn Bickmore and EAAC, who were convinced that Tyler had masterminded the bombings in an effort to halt environmental destruction.

"And I haven't given up," she stated firmly, though part of her was scared, too. Four of Kreig's hired thugs had tried to kill them just for snooping. What would they have done to a college kid who threatened to go to the police?

Allison looked at her, tears glistening. "I just keep trying to figure out how they could have gotten Tyler's signature on those bomb threats. It just doesn't make sense."

"No, it doesn't, unless—wait a minute!" Excited, Nancy grasped Allison's wrist. Suddenly it *did* make sense. "Unless Tyler didn't disappear on his own. What if he was kidnapped and *forced* to write those letters."

"Kidnapped?" Allison's mouth fell open. "That would explain why he just vanished without a word. But forced to write the letters?" She frowned uncertainly. "I can't see Tyler bowing to pressure. He'd be the kind of guy who would say, 'Go ahead and kill me. I don't care.'"

"Yes, but what if whoever kidnapped him threatened to kill *you?*"

"Me?" Allison pointed to herself in astonishment.

Nancy nodded eagerly. "I couldn't figure out why you were attacked on the ski slope, but now it makes sense. They needed your cap to show Tyler that they could get close enough to kill you anytime, anywhere."

"Wow." George exhaled loudly. "That's ruthless."

Together, the two of them stared at Allison as they realized how vulnerable their friend was.

Nancy jumped up. "I'm going to try to page the Hardys. I doubt the police will buy into our theory, but Joe and Frank will. When we get to the dedication, I want to make sure they're guarding *you,* too, Allison."

"And thanks to public and private efforts, the Sports Park, home of the upcoming Winter Games, is turning into a world-class facility,"

Horst Kreig said, his voice ringing over loud-speakers. Standing on the top of the bobsled run, Kreig was addressing a crowd of over a hundred politicians, reporters, and interested civilians.

"And Utah will go down in the history books when it hosts the next Olympic Games," he added, punching the air with his fist. The crowd erupted in whistles and applause.

Nancy clapped politely. Searching the perimeter of the crowd, she spotted Joe, who was talking into a portable radio. When he saw Nancy, he came over.

"I'm keeping my eye on you," he told Allison. Just then, a weasel-like man bustled up. He wore muddy workboots crusted with a black substance and a jacket with a security guard emblem. "Hardy, I told you to keep on the perimeter of the crowd."

"Right, boss. Nancy, this is Roger Weems, head of security."

Weems barely nodded before rushing off. "Well, I'd better get to work before Weems has a coronary." Joe winked at the girls, then strolled back the way he'd come.

"Look!" George poked Nancy in the ribs to get her attention. "There's Detective Urich and another officer standing behind Horst Kreig. I'm going to enjoy the look on Kreig's face when he's handcuffed and taken away."

Taking a pair of scissors, Kreig stepped forward and cut the ceremonial ribbon. Then he raised both hands in triumph as the crowd again applauded. At the same time Detective Urich came up beside him and said loudly enough for everyone to hear over the microphone, "Horst Kreig, you are under arrest for conspiracy to commit murder—"

The rest of his words were drowned out by the shouts and calls of reporters. People behind Nancy surged forward to get a better look. Linking her arm with Allison's, she pulled her friend away from the milling crowd.

When she turned back to see what was going on, she saw a man in a ski parka break away from the crowd and take off at a run toward the parking lot. She recognized him instantly— James Kreig!

"George! It's James Kreig, Horst Kreig's son. And for some reason he's in a big hurry."

"We can't let him get away!" Allison said, starting in his direction. "Quick, find a security guard."

"No!" Nancy stopped Allison. Her eyes were wide and she was breathing hard as her mind raced with possibilities. "What if Kreig has Tyler? He might be able to lead us to him."

Wildly, Nancy hunted for the Hardys and found Joe first. She grabbed his wrist. "Come on."

"What?" Joe looked startled. "I can't leave my post."

"But James Kreig is getting away. George, find Frank. Have him follow us. Joe will keep in radio contact." Still holding Joe, Nancy began to run toward the parking lot. She didn't want to lose Kreig. "Allison, you stay here," she shouted.

"No way! Not if this involves Tyler."

Nancy didn't have time to argue. She, Joe, and Allison pounded across the gravel drive and jumped into Allison's car.

"Now, tell me what we're doing," Joe said as Allison shifted into third and sped away from the lot.

"We're hoping Kreig's son is going to lead us to Tyler Conklin." Nancy told Joe her theory about Tyler's being kidnapped and forced to write the bomb threats.

"Don't you see?" Allison exclaimed. "It's the only thing that makes sense!"

"I hope so," Joe muttered as Allison wound dizzily through traffic, keeping Kreig in sight. Turning on his radio, Joe called Frank. George had just found him and told him what was going on. Together, they'd located Kip and were headed after them.

A tense twenty minutes later, Nancy realized they were going through Park City, where Kip's family lived. Allison had maintained a safe distance behind Kreig's car, which was traveling at a determined pace.

Then, without warning, Kreig turned off onto a gravel road. Allison slowed, then turned to follow. Since it was a one-lane road with no traffic, Nancy knew they'd be easily spotted.

"Stay way behind," she warned from the backseat. Joe hunted for landmarks to relay back to Frank, George, and Kip. "There's a gas station, a stand of pines, and an old sign. Wait a minute, Frank. Do you remember when we went over those printouts last night from the Bureau of Land Development?"

"Right," Frank's voice squawked back. "American Progress owned a lot of mines. Some abandoned."

"Well, I think we're about to explore one of them. The Kay-Two mine."

Sitting forward, Nancy listened eagerly.

"Kay-Two. Wasn't that the old silver mine?" Frank asked.

"Right."

"Why is Kreig heading there?"

"Nancy has a hunch they've got Tyler Conklin stashed there. We'll soon find out." Joe signed off just as the road opened into a cleared area surrounded by trees.

"Stop back here in the trees," Nancy said.

In the distance she could see Kreig's car parked in front of the entrance to a mine. It was barred with a padlock on a metal gate. After unlocking the padlock, he opened the gate and slipped a hand inside his jacket to pull out a gun.

Nancy inhaled deeply. "Oh, no! They *must* have Tyler stashed in there. And now that Horst

Kreig's been arrested, they don't have any use for him anymore."

"You mean they're going to kill him?" Allison cried, her voice rising hysterically.

"Not if I can help it!" Nancy declared. Throwing open the car door, she bolted toward the mine.

Chapter

Seventeen

Nancy! Wait!" Joe scrambled from the car. James Kreig had vanished into the mine, so fortunately, he hadn't seen Nancy charge across the snowy clearing.

"He'll kill her!" Allison panted as she raced behind Joe. "Then he'll kill Tyler!"

"Not if we get to him first." Skidding to a stop, Joe ducked around the metal gate. Nancy had halted inside the beamed cave. Dim lights set into the wall lit a wooden stairway that seemed to go down forever. Narrow railroad tracks bisected the tunnel.

Nancy was about to head down the stairs when Joe grabbed her arm. "Slow down, Nan, or you're going to announce to Kreig that we're here. We have to be quiet."

Taking a deep breath, Nancy nodded. "You're right. Especially since we don't know the layout of the mine."

Allison shuddered. "This place is creepy. I can't imagine Tyler being forced to stay here." She turned worriedly to Nancy. "Do you think he's okay?"

"We know he must still be alive or Kreig wouldn't be in such a hurry. Look, Joe, we can't wait for Frank and the others. We've got to get to Kreig before he gets to Tyler."

"Right," Joe agreed, though he realized what they were doing—heading into the depths of a dark, abandoned mine—was crazy. Stepping back toward the gate, he tried to reach Frank one more time. There was no answer.

"We lost contact." After turning off the radio, he stuck it in his pocket. He just hoped that Frank would be right behind them.

"Okay." Nancy took a deep breath. "We'll head down the stairs. Stay absolutely silent and keep your eyes peeled for any sign of Kreig. In order to take him, we're going to have to surprise him."

"Sounds good." Joe led the way. The stairs were slick and many of the boards had rotted.

When they reached the bottom of the stairs, the tunnel opened into two passages. One was lighted, the other dark. Where had Kreig gone?

Then Joe saw a flicker in the darker passage, as

if someone was moving down it carrying a flashlight. The tracks also led into that tunnel.

Joe pulled his flashlight from his equipment belt and signaled the girls to follow him. For the first time, he wished that Weems had issued guns to the guards.

As he walked through the tunnel, he cast the light back and forth, hunting for a weapon. When the beam reflected off something metal, Joe bent down to look closer. It was a rusty hammer.

Perfect.

Feeling a little better, Joe worked his way deeper into the tunnel. He walked slowly. Behind him, Allison and Nancy stumbled often, but Joe was afraid to aim the light in too wide an arc in case Kreig glanced back.

The tunnel took a sharp turn. Beyond it, Joe could see the glow of light. He flicked off his flashlight, then sneaked forward. Flattening himself against the mine wall, he peered around some jutting rock.

James Kreig stood beside what looked like a small box on wheels. A mining car, Joe figured. Inside the car, a guy about his own age was slumped forward, his long, tangled hair hanging in his eyes. From what Joe could see, his mouth wasn't taped, but his hands must have been bound behind him.

"No one's ever going to find your body, Conklin," Kreig was saying as he pressed the gun barrel to Tyler's temple. "They'll figure you ran scared after your last bomb threat and disappeared to Mexico or some foreign place you radical hippies like to go."

"What about Allison?" Tyler asked, his lips barely moving.

Kreig shrugged. "Pavin's arranged for her and that nosy friend of hers to have a nasty accident. Only this time, he'll make sure neither of them survive."

"No!" Tyler struggled feebly against his bonds, but Joe could tell he'd had most of the fight wiped out of him. He also knew he had to do something fast.

"Put down your gun, Kreig," Joe shouted. "This is the police. We have you surrounded!"

Kreig spun around, his gun pointing in Joe's direction. "Never!" he shouted, shooting three times.

The roar of the shots was deafening, echoing through the mine like blasts of dynamite. Above Joe, rock crumbled and beams groaned. Were the shots going to bring down the tunnel?

The hum of a motor made Joe look back toward Kreig. The man had leaped into a mining car. It must have been motorized because he took off down the track, heading away from Joe and deeper into the mine.

"Stay here and help Tyler!" Joe shouted to Allison and Nancy. Springing into action, he leaped into a second mining car. Still holding the hammer, he found the On button and the throttle. He started the motor and headed down the tracks. A clanging noise up ahead told him that Kreig had had a pretty good head start. But that wasn't going to keep Joe from catching him.

"Quick! Untie Tyler's ankles!" Nancy shouted as she raced into the circle of light shed by a Coleman lantern. "The tunnel's going to cave in!"

Rushing forward, she and Allison reached Tyler.

"Are you all right!" Allison sobbed as she fumbled at the ropes around her boyfriend's ankles. Tipping him forward, Nancy worked on the ropes binding his wrists. Beams creaked and chunks of rock spilled down from the ceiling. They didn't have much time.

When Tyler was unbound, he pulled his arms in front of him and rubbed his wrists. In the dim light, Nancy could see bone-weary fatigue etched across his face. Would he make it out?

The mining car! Quickly, she picked up the lantern and looked into the car, hunting for some way to start it. But a quick glance told her this was an old car, not motorized. They were on their own.

"Allison." Nancy's voice was sharp. A flurry of stone cascaded on top of her head. "Tyler's going to need our help making it to the entrance."

Allison nodded and Nancy saw a glint of

determination return to her friend's eyes. Together, they lifted Tyler to a standing position. His legs buckled, but with a grunt of effort, he pulled himself up and climbed from the car.

"Hurry!" Nancy's heart pounded as a rumble filled her ears. Flanking Tyler, they half-carried, half-guided him down the passage toward the entrance. Nancy carried the lantern to light the way, though it banged painfully against her knees with each step.

Behind her, she heard the thunderous crack of wood and crash of rock. Allison screamed. The two girls broke into a run, Tyler stumbling between them. The lantern whacked against the wall, shattering, and the tunnel was plunged into darkness.

"Get down!" Nancy yelled. Diving forward, the three flattened themselves on the mine floor, their hands over their heads.

For what seemed like forever, the cave echoed with the sounds of falling rock. Stone and dust rained down on top of Nancy, pelting her like hail. Then, just as suddenly, all was quiet.

Cautiously, she looked up and noticed immediately that there was some light. They'd landed at the bottom of the stairs, where a few bulbs still shone feebly. Beside her, Tyler and Allison were stirring.

"Everyone okay?" Nancy asked.

Allison answered for both of them. "Yes, we're okay."

Nancy sat up and peered down the tunnel they'd just come up. It was completely blocked. Unless there was another exit at the other end, Joe was sealed in the mine.

"Nancy!" Someone was at the top of the steps. Scrambling to her feet, Nancy saw Frank, George, and Kip pounding down the stairs toward them.

"Thank goodness you're all right!" George exclaimed, hugging Nancy when she reached her. Allison and Tyler were still sitting on the rubble-strewn mine floor. Allison's arms were supporting Tyler, and they were both covered with dirt and dust.

"What happened?" Frank's gaze darted from the blocked tunnel to Nancy's face. "Where's Joe?"

Tears filled Nancy's eyes. "He went after James Kreig." She gestured toward the wall of rock that blocked the passageway. "We were in the tunnel. When we found Tyler, Kreig shot at us. It started the cave-in." A lump filled her throat.

Frank, George, and Kip were staring at her in shocked silence. "Kreig jumped in a mining car and headed in the opposite direction," she continued. "Joe went after him. We made a run for it."

"There's got to be another way out," Frank declared.

"There is," Tyler said, his voice cracking.

"Kreig and the other guy would come in from both entrances."

Frank, George, and Kip all looked down at Tyler.

Allison grinned up at them. "Tyler Conklin, meet the best bunch of detectives—and friends—a girl could have."

After Allison had introduced everybody, Nancy asked Tyler, "There were two guys?"

"Right. Only one of them never said a word. He'd bring me a sandwich and a glass of water, then leave." Wearily, he rubbed his hand over his forehead. "Man, you guys showed up just in time. I thought I was dead."

Suddenly it hit Nancy who the other guy was. She remembered hiding under the bed at Tyler's apartment and watching work boots stomp past—boots covered in black mining dust.

She had just seen those same boots at the dedication. "Weems is the other guy. He's in on it, too," she said abruptly.

"Weems!" Kip and Frank chorused.

"It makes perfect sense. He was able to tip off Pavin or Kreig about you and Joe, about security at the Sports Park—everything!" Nancy's brows shot up. "Does he know you're here?"

"No. We split too fast, and he was preoccupied with the police arresting Horst Kreig and the possibility of another bomb."

"A bomb that I never planted," Tyler said ruefully. "They kept saying they'd kill Allison if I didn't follow their orders. At first I didn't believe them. But then they brought me her ski cap, and I knew . . . ." His voice faltered. Allison gave his hand a squeeze.

"We finally figured out you were forced to sign those letters," Nancy said. "Though Allison never gave up on you."

"If Pavin doesn't know we're here, and James Kreig didn't call in reinforcements, then we'll be okay," Frank said. "Now we just have to find that other entrance."

"I've got a bunch of maps in the Jeep that might help," Kip said. "A lot of cavers like to explore mines. Kay-Two might be on one of the maps."

"Great." Frank cuffed Kip on the arm before starting up the steps. "Come on. We have a mine entrance to find and a Hardy to save."

Joe strained his eyes, trying to see the car ahead of him. A few lights winked from the walls, but mostly the tunnel was dark.

"Kreig!" Joe hollered over the rumble of the wheels on the track. "Give it up!"

The sound of gunfire made him duck down in the car. That was Kreig's fourth shot, which meant he had one or two rounds left, depending on the type of revolver.

The car whipped around a curve, throwing Joe sideways. Then the tunnel grew lighter. He scrunched lower. He felt like a sitting duck.

Ahead, he saw the end of Kreig's car fly around the corner. When it disappeared, he sat up straight. The tracks were coming to an end. Joe breathed a sigh of relief when he noticed light pouring in from behind a wooden barricade. Gravel dust was mounded in front of it. At least they'd been heading for an exit.

Kreig rocketed down the hill toward the end, braked his car, and jumped out. Turning, the gunman fired one last time and missed. Then, to Joe's relief, Kreig fled. He was either out of bullets or he'd believed Joe's lie about the police surrounding the place.

Joe's relief turned into horror when he reached for the handbrake and pulled. It didn't budge. A sign dangling from the ceiling warned, "USE BRAKES. NEXT QUARTER-MILE DOWN-HILL TO END OF LINE."

Joe pulled on the handbrake again, his mind flashing to the bobsled tearing down the run. Only now he was riding in a metal box of a car with no steering and a jammed brake, and he was barreling toward a high wooden wall.

If he didn't do something quick, he was going to be smashed like a bug on a windshield.

Chapter

Eighteen

THE HAMMER WAS still clutched in Joe's hand. Maybe he could unjam the brake with it.

As the car raced toward the barricade, Joe held the tool with both hands and whacked the brake. It popped to the right. With a screech of metal on metal, the car jolted to a stop. Joe flew forward, hit the front of the car, and flipped onto the pile of gravel dust.

He landed hard, but not as hard as if he'd dead-centered the wooden wall. "Ooo." Rubbing his backside, he got to his feet. With a groan, he jogged around the wall to the exit, wincing with each step. He must have hit his knee when he fell.

He was just in time to see Kreig sprinting down a snowy road. The man was about two hundred yards ahead and running fast. Joe knew there was no way he was going to catch him.

Then the roar of a motor made Kreig stop in his tracks. Kip's Jeep was charging up the road, right for Kreig. The man dove off the road to avoid the vehicle, then took off into a sparse pine woods.

Kip, Frank, and George spilled from the Jeep and took off after Kreig.

When Joe finally limped up to Kreig, he was lying facedown in the dirt. Kip was kneeling on one shoulder, bending Kreig's arm back. Frank was on the other, and George had a big tree limb in her hand, ready to strike.

"I'll use my radio to call the police," Joe said.

"No!" Frank blurted out. "Weems might pick up on the transmission. We don't want him to run."

"Weems?"

"He's in on this, too," Frank explained. "Nancy's gone to a pay phone to call Detective Urich, then the Park City police. They should be here any minute."

"So they got Tyler out all right?" Joe asked.

"Yup." Still holding Kreig, Frank glanced over at his brother and grinned. When Joe looked down, he realized he was covered with dust. "They looked as bad as you, too. The mine caved in."

"Thank goodness they got out in time." Suddenly tired, Joe sank to the ground. "Is Tyler going to be okay?"

"Yes," George said. "He's suffering from exhaustion."

"I know how he feels," Joe muttered. He looked at James Kreig. The heir to the largest corporation in Utah had his cheek pressed in the dirt. "So why'd you and your dad do it?" he asked him. "Didn't you have enough money?"

"Money?" Kreig gave a sharp bark, his voice distorted by his awkward position. "Don't you know, kid? It's all about power and taking risks. Money's just one of the benefits."

Power, huh? Joe shook his head. Kreig and his dad wouldn't have much power in jail.

"Only this time your risks didn't pay off," Frank said. "Your dad's been arrested, and it won't be long before Senator Pavin and Roger Weems join him. In fact, I'd say a bunch of teen detectives toppled your powerful empire."

Kreig humphed. "Just watch. My dad's lawyers will get me out in no time."

Joe and Frank exchanged glances. Kreig had no idea the trouble he was in.

"I'm afraid this time your 'daddy' isn't going to be able to bail you out," Kip said sarcastically.

"I'm just glad it's over," Joe said. "I'm ready for a vacation. How about a day of skiing tomorrow?" he asked Kip.

"Sounds good to me."

"And me," George chimed in. "I plan to spend

my last day on the slopes." She gave Kip a big grin. Joe smiled, too, thinking about Shana and how he'd love to spend his last day with her.

Joe's radio crackled at the same time Frank's did. He pulled it from his jacket pocket and turned it on. He could hear Weems hollering, "All guards proceed to the ski jump. A bomb just exploded!"

What in the world is going on? Frank thought as he, Kip, George, and Joe sped back toward the Sports Park. As soon as the local police had arrived to take custody of Kreig, the four had gone off after assuring the confused cops that Detective Urich would explain everything.

Joe sat in the backseat with George, his radio on. Frank could hear the frantic shouting of the guards. Even Weems was yelling. From what Frank could tell from the garbled transmission, the bomb had exploded at the end of the ski jump.

"Baker, check the first floor of the tower," Weems was ordering. "We don't know if there are others set to go—"

Frank heard a loud boom, then Weems's hysterical cry, "There was another one!" Then the radio went dead.

Frank met Joe's horrified gaze. "What's going on?" his brother stammered. "I thought we had everybody."

"Unless Kreig's thugs are exacting revenge," George said.

"I can't imagine that happening," Kip said. "Kreig and his lawyers are probably smooth-talking and plea-bargaining their way out of a big jail sentence right now. Something like this would turn the public so much against Kreig and American Progress the company would never recover."

"But then who?" Frank repeated.

"We're almost to the ski jump," Kip replied. "We'll soon find out."

Kip drove up the winding road to the ski area and parked in the crowded lot at the foot of the mountain. Curious spectators were streaming in. A line of police officers wearing orange vests over their uniforms was holding them back.

Frank pulled on his coat, then climbed from the Jeep, his security guard badge in hand. Joe had already identified himself and was jogging toward the ski jump. Kip and George had left to find a better spot to view the excitement.

"Frank!"

Nancy jogged over to him. "What's going on?" she demanded. "Didn't you catch Kreig?"

"Yes. We left him with the local police." He glanced over Nancy's head. "Where are Tyler and Allison?"

"They went to get something to eat—all Tyler could talk about was a juicy burger—then they had to go back to the police station. They're both waiting to be interviewed by Urich. Later, Tyler has to identify James Kreig from a lineup. But with this fiasco, it may take a while. Half the police force is here."

" 'Fiasco' is right." Frank ran his fingers through his hair.

"Do you think Robyn Bickmore and EAAC are responsible for this?" Nancy asked.

"Could be. Except that Weems and the police were watching them like hawks, so I don't know how they could have sneaked in here."

"Weems." Nancy snorted. "You mean the crook who's in cahoots with Pavin? Maybe he *let* them in."

"I can't imagine he has anything to do with what's happening right now. Look, I've got to get in there and help." He started toward the police line. Nancy fell into step beside him.

"And I'm going with you."

"Too dangerous. Besides, how do you plan on getting past the mounties?"

"Just watch."

As Frank showed his badge to an officer, Nancy clutched his arm. "I think I know the bomber!" she cried, her voice rising hysterically. "Please, let me through. I can talk to him!"

The officer looked at Frank. "She could help," he assured him—not lying, but not telling the truth exactly.

"Go on in." The officer stepped aside. Nancy and Frank rushed up the snowy slope toward the landing area of the ski jump. When they saw the destruction, they both stopped dead.

The whole end of the ski jump had been blown clean off, flinging concrete and steel everywhere. Already, bomb-squad experts were collecting evidence and workers were cleaning up.

Frank stopped one of the security guards. "Where was the second blast?"

"Tower." The guy jerked his head in that direction. "Second floor. They've got the bomber trapped in there."

"It's just one guy?"

"Yeah."

"Do they know who it is?"

The guard shook his head. "I don't know. I've been down here most of the time helping collect evidence. They're trying to find all the pieces of the bomb. Our radios went out so communication is dead," he added as he hurried off.

"If it was one guy, that blows our EAAC theory," Nancy said as she and Frank jogged toward the tower.

"Not necessarily. Bickmore could have sent some zealous club member on a suicide mission. As I recall, they're all slightly crazy."

When they reached the double doors leading into the tower, a guard stopped them. When he recognized Frank, he let the two of them through.

"It's wild up there," the guard said. "The guy's got a bomb taped to him."

"A bomb!"

"So no one can take him down."

"Do they know who it is?"

"He was wearing a black ski mask, so no one's identified him yet. And what's even worse, he has a hostage."

"Who?" Nancy asked.

"Don't know."

Dashing inside, Nancy and Frank pushed past milling guards, police officers, and officials and went upstairs. When they came out into the second-floor lobby area, Joe met them.

"Things are crazy," he told them. "The guy's holed up in a supply room. It's got no windows and only one door, so no one can see a thing, and because the radios are down, no one seems to know what's going on."

"What about police radios?" Frank asked.

"Something seems to have jammed their frequency. Whoever planned this bombing was prepared."

Just then Weems bustled down the corridor toward them. Frank stopped him. He could barely look the guy in the face, but he knew that now was not the time to talk about his role in Tyler's kidnapping.

But Nancy had no misgivings. "Hey, Weems," she called, her tone combative. "Been down in the Kay-Two mine lately?"

All the blood rushed from the man's face. "What—what are you talking about?" he stammered.

Stepping up to him, Joe poked a finger at Weems's chest. "She's talking about kidnapping. Gee, Nancy, how many years do you get these days for kidnapping?"

"Maybe the rest of your life," Nancy said grimly.

Weems seemed to collapse with the weight of their accusation. "Look," he said in a low voice, "I wasn't in on the kidnapping. James Kreig had me take food down to the boy. That's all."

"Oh, I don't think that's quite all," Nancy said. "How about helping Pavin search Tyler's apartment?"

"And blowing our cover," Frank added angrily, not about to let Weems off the hook now that Nancy had started the accusations. "You told Kreig and Pavin our every move. That's how that thug knew Joe and I were guarding the ski jump that night. They must have followed us to the warehouse, too. They set the third floor on fire, Weems. Did you know that? You almost got us killed!"

"All right, I admit I told them," Weems croaked. He gestured for the three to follow him into a deserted room. "But I only told them where you'd be working. From the beginning, Pavin knew you two were detectives. In fact, he was the one who suggested hiring you. He never figured two teenagers would catch on to his scam."

"Which one?" Joe prodded. "Seems he was double-dealing everybody."

"I don't know all the details. All I know is that Pavin was paying me to look the other way when the sabotage started. The plan was to make it look like some radical environmental group was responsible. He said the state was sick of the environmentalists blocking projects and development. He figured that if groups like EAAC were exposed by the media as a bunch of nuts, the public would quit supporting them."

"And you bought into that?" Nancy asked.

"Look, if I knew Pavin was working with that shark Horst Kreig, I never would have helped him," Weems insisted. "When I found out how ruthless the two were, I tried to back out. But it was too late. They threatened my wife and kids if I didn't cooperate." Anxiously, he ran his hand over his face.

Frank almost felt sorry for him. *Almost.* "You're a cowardly worm, Weems. When you saw they had kidnapped Tyler, you must have known something else was going on. You should have notified the police."

"You're right. I should have. But by then I was in too deep," Weems explained. "Pavin told me Tyler was going to expose him. He and Kreig were almost gleeful when they devised a way to use Tyler in their scheme. They'd get him to sign threatening letters. That way the police and the media would have to go after him and groups like EAAC."

"Only Tyler wouldn't sign the letters, would he," Nancy said.

Weems nodded wearily. "Until James Kreig said he'd kill Tyler's girlfriend, Allison, if he didn't cooperate. James has always been a loose cannon. Even his father wasn't able to control him. From there, things escalated."

"Well, their greedy empire has crumbled," Joe said. "Both Kreigs have been arrested. If I were you, Weems, I'd turn myself in."

"Joe! Frank!" Walt Coles rushed into the room. Frank swung around in surprise.

Kip's uncle's face was ashen. "It's Shana!"

"Shana?" Joe grabbed the sleeve of Walt's coat. "What are you talking about?"

"Todd Ellman's got her. He's the bomber. And he's holding her hostage!"

Chapter

Nineteen

Todd Ellman? The contractor?" Frank repeated in astonishment.

Uncle Walt's shoulders slumped. "I should have known it was Ellman who bombed the bobsled run. He was furious when I got a contract and he didn't. Everybody was just pointing the finger at those environmentalists, so I didn't suspect him. But then when you brought me that letter and those bids from his office, there was the proof right in front of me. . . ." His voice failed. "Oh, why didn't I figure it out!"

Joe clutched his arm. "How'd Shana get involved?"

"It was all my fault!" Uncle Walt covered his face with his callused hands. "He came over at noon, wanting to apply for a job. I sent him back to the trailer with Shana to get an application. When I returned for lunch, they were gone. I just assumed she'd left to eat. But he must have grabbed her then."

"That was several hours ago!" Nancy gasped. "He must have been holding her all this time."

Frank smacked his fist against his palm. "I'll bet he used her to get past security and into the ski-jump area. I mean, all the crew knows Shana. They must not have suspected anything."

"Why'd it take so long to find out she was the hostage?" Nancy asked.

Walt shook his head. "The police only contacted me about twenty minutes ago. I rushed right up here."

"When Ellman jammed all the radios, communication broke down," Weems explained, some of the authority creeping back into his voice. Frank knew that despite what Weems had done, the head of security still had a job to do. "Then, when the first bomb went off, pandemonium broke out. We think he may have had her stashed in a closet the whole time—to use as a hostage in case he didn't escape."

One of the guards bustled up, a roll of papers in his hand. "Here are the blueprints of the building," he told Weems.

"Just in time." Weems unrolled them. After scanning several, he tapped the middle of the second one. "Here's where he has Shana. We plan to cut a hole in this wall so we can grab her and get her out before the bomb squad rushes Ellman."

Uncle Walt tensed. "Isn't that risky? Won't he hear you?"

Weems rolled the blueprints back up. "We'll do everything we can to make sure Ellman doesn't hear us go through the wall. But we're afraid if we don't do something fast, he's going to lose it and set that bomb off."

"Please, you've got to save my daughter," Uncle Walt pleaded.

Weems gave his shoulder a squeeze. "I'll do everything I can," he promised, adding, "It's not like I've got anything to lose." He straightened. "Frank, you keep the other guards informed. Joe, come with me. Let's go disarm a bomber."

When Joe left, Nancy turned to Frank. "I'm not about to sit back and do nothing. I've got an idea in case Weems's plan fails."

"And I want to hear it." Frank looked at Walt. "I'm sorry. Joe and I should have followed our hunches on Ellman," he apologized. "We got distracted by the Kreigs. Maybe Nancy and I can make it up to you by making sure Shana gets out of this okay."

Hope glimmered in Walt's eyes. "I have more confidence in you two than in the police. They never even suspected Ellman. Do whatever you have to do to save my daughter. I'm going to find Kip and tell him what's going on." He sighed. "I guess I better tell my wife, too. Before she hears it on the news."

When he left, Nancy linked her arm through Frank's and walked with him to a quiet corner.

"According to Weems and Joe," she began, "Shana is stashed in a supply closet with only one door—which Ellman is blocking—and no windows. But what about vents?"

She pointed over her head. "Most of these large buildings have complicated systems for heating and cooling installed in the ceiling. I bet this one does, too, since it has a dropped ceiling with light panels. There might be some way to reach Shana from above."

Frank grinned. "Nancy, you're a genuis."

"Not quite. We have to figure out how to sneak her out once we get to her."

"We'll figure that out as we go."

Pushing her way through the crowd, Nancy led Frank to a deserted room in the back of the second floor. "I got a good look at the blueprints over Weems's shoulder so I know right where the supply closet is located. I just hope we can find it once we're in the ceiling, crawling along in the dark."

"If Weems's crew is making enough noise to keep Ellman from hearing them cut a hole in the wall, we should be able to locate Shana and Ellman with no problem."

Nancy nodded absently, her mind still on how they were going to lift Shana out. Her gaze alighted on a rope coiled in the corner of the room. "Bingo."

Grinning, she picked it up and showed it to Frank. He smiled back, then found two boxes of paint cans. When he stacked them on top of each other and climbed up, he was tall enough to push the ceiling panel out.

Grabbing two of the wooden joists, he pulled himself up. For a second he disappeared, then Nancy saw his face in the opening. "Think you can pull yourself up?" he asked.

"Hey, I didn't win the Most Chin-ups Award for nothing," Nancy joked as she threw the rope to him. He coiled it around his shoulder, then helped her climb up. She immediately banged her head.

"Ow!" She rubbed the spot.

Frank put a finger to his lips. "Which way?"

Nancy pictured the blueprints in her mind, then started off to the right. Since they had to crawl on the narrow wooden joists, avoiding the various wires, the going was slow.

"My knees are going to have permanent dents," Frank whispered behind her. Nancy could only nod in agreement. Stopping, she listened for a minute. Someone was playing the news on the radio. Or was it the news?

Someone speaking sounded like a TV commentator. Nancy heard him ask a question, then a different voice answered loudly and angrily.

They must have gotten someone to interview

Ellman, she thought. Maybe that's what the guy wanted all along. Hopefully it would distract him long enough for someone to save Shana.

The voices grew louder as Nancy neared the ceiling of the supply closet. She could hear the reporter's questions loud and clear; he must have been using a microphone. Was the whole thing being broadcast live?

"So you blame this all on Senator Pavin?" the reporter was asking.

"Darn right. Pavin ruined me and lots of others. I'm not just doing this for me. I'm doing it for every working stiff who's been cheated by lying government officials."

Nancy waved to Frank. She was pretty sure they were over the supply closet. Slowly and carefully, he helped her remove the ceiling panel. When she peered into the dim room, she could see Shana huddled in the corner. A gag was in her mouth and her hands and ankles were bound with duct tape.

Nancy's heart plunked to her toes. They'd have to free her before they could get her out. Would they be able to without Ellman hearing?

She glanced over at Ellman. He stood in the doorway, his back to his hostage. His arms were waving wildly as he went on and on about corrupt officials. If only the reporter could keep him talking.

Just then Shana looked up. When she saw Nancy, her eyes filled with tears of hope. Nancy glanced back at Ellman. Several sticks of dynamite were strapped to his leg. Wires led from the dynamite to something in his hand. The detonator?

Ellman's voice rose. Nancy could tell he was getting more agitated. They might not have much time before he went off the deep end.

Nancy looked at Frank. For a second, they stared at each other. She knew he was thinking the same thing—they had to take the chance.

Before Frank could make a move, Nancy grabbed the two joists and swung down into the room. Pulling a penknife from her pocket, she crept over to Shana and cut the tape around her wrists and ankles.

Frank had lowered the rope. Shana grabbed it. Nancy boosted her from below, while Frank pulled from above. In an instant, Shana disappeared into the dark cave of the ceiling.

Nancy was about to reach for the rope when Ellman began to turn. She froze. He was going to catch her!

Suddenly she heard the reporter holler shrilly as if he'd noticed what was going on and knew he had to distract Ellman. "Sir, Horst Kreig is the one you should be mad at. He's the mastermind behind all the swindles."

"Kreig!" Ellman thundered as he turned back toward the reporter. "Let me tell you what I know about that money-grubbing barracuda."

The rope dropped onto Nancy's shoulder and

she grabbed hold. Kicking her legs, she climbed up. Frank and Shana each grasped a wrist and hoisted her next to them.

As Nancy caught her breath, Shana peeled the tape from her mouth. "Thanks," she whispered.

Frank gestured that they didn't have much time. Quickly, he led them back the way they'd come.

Nancy heard Ellman bellow, "This is my final message to corrupt businessmen and officials. This is what your greed drove me to!"

What was Ellman going to do? Nancy's heart pounded as she crawled as fast as she could after Shana and Frank.

The reporter began to cry out, "No! Don't do it!"

Ellman was going to set off the bomb!

Chapter
Twenty

"No!" Joe bellowed from inside the helmet of his bomb suit. "Get out of the way! He's going to blow!"

Pushing the reporter out of the way, he and Weems, also in a bomb suit, dove for Ellman. But they were too late. With a macabre grin, Ellman pressed the detonator.

The blast propelled Joe twenty feet in the air. He could hear screaming and shouting and a roar like a thousand jets revving up, then all was silent.

"Joe?" Someone was bent over him, calling his name. Joe blinked. Big blue eyes the color of the sky stared at him from the most beautiful face he'd ever seen. He reached up to touch the creamy white cheek.

"Are you an angel?" he asked.

"No, it's Shana."

Joe blinked again, trying to focus. "Shana? Then you are an angel." Reaching behind her head, he pulled her close for a kiss. Several people laughed.

Joe tilted his chin to look around. Frank, Nancy, Uncle Walt, Kip, and George were grouped at his feet in a semicircle. He struggled to sit up, but his body felt so heavy, he knew he must be paralyzed or mortally wounded.

"How long do I have to live?" he whispered.

"About seventy more years," Shana guessed.

"You mean, I'm not dying?"

She shook her head. "Of course not. The medic said you'll be fine."

"Then why can't I move?"

"Because you're still wearing an eighty-five-pound bomb suit."

"I am?" Joe lifted a leg to check for himself. On the end was a strange-looking black boot. Shana was right. Relieved, Joe plunked his head back on the floor. "What about Weems?"

Frank squatted beside Joe. "He's got several broken ribs. The medics are working on him now. Too bad they'll just get him fixed up so he can go to jail."

"Yeah. But the guy did risk his life. Maybe he's

not such a mouse after all." Joe closed his eyes a second. His ears were still ringing from the blast. "And what about Ellman?" he finally asked.

Shana ducked her chin in sorrow. Frank shook his head. "Let's just say Kreig and Pavin can add murder to their list of crimes, if we can prove they drove Ellman to kill himself."

"Wow." Joe blew out a breath and took Shana's hand in his. "Hey, Frank, thanks for getting Shana out of that room in time."

Frank gestured for Nancy to come over. "It was all Detective Drew's idea."

"Thanks, Nan."

"All in a day's work," she joked.

Joe rubbed his forehead. "I'm going to have a splitting headache."

"I think the medics better check you again," Frank said, smiling down at him. "We want you in tiptop shape for tomorrow."

"Tomorrow?" Joe was confused. "Didn't we catch all the bad guys?"

"We did," Nancy assured him. "Tomorrow we've got an even bigger challenge—fresh powder in the Wasatch Mountains!"

"Whooo-hooo!" Kip and George shouted as they whizzed down the slope on snowboards.

The two held hands as they zoomed past Nancy and Frank. Then Kip lost his balance and, flying through the air, plowed into a snowbank.

George bailed off her snowboard and fell into the bank beside him. "Try it, you two couch potatoes!" she challenged.

Nancy lifted one brow. "What do you think, Frank?" The two were sitting on an outcropping of rock, resting after a morning of skiing.

"I think I'm going to finish this hot chocolate and count my bruises from my encounter with that avalanche. If I have under fifty, I'll race you."

She grinned. "You're on."

Just then, Joe and Shana came across the mountainside. The two had skied cross-country from Shana's car, which was parked downhill. Joe's face was bright red, and sweat rolled down his forehead. Shana grinned and waved happily. Her hair wasn't even messy.

"I don't think Shana even broke a sweat!" Joe hollered when they were close enough. He glided to a stop. "That's hard work! I'll take downhill skiing anytime."

"Wimp." Shana punched him on the chest. With a dramatic groan, Joe threw his arms wide and fell flat in the snow. His skis and poles stuck up every which way.

Nancy, Frank, and Shana laughed.

"Does that mean you're ready for a lunch break?" Shana teased.

Nancy patted the backpack. "There are plenty of turkey sandwiches—compliments of Kip's mom, who says she has lots of leftovers from Thanksgiving. Plus hot chocolate, oranges, brownies . . ."

"Brownies!" Joe popped up. "Umm. Hand me about ten of those devils. I worked up an appetite."

"Feeling okay, Joe?" Nancy asked as she passed out brownies to everybody. George and Kip were trudging up the hill for another run on the snowboards.

"Feeling great. Nothing like a bomb blast to clear your head." He glanced at Frank. "Maybe we should have whacked ourselves earlier. A clear head would have made us finger Ellman right off. Then Shana wouldn't have been taken hostage. And he never would have blown up the ski jump or killed himself."

"It wasn't all our fault, Joe," Frank reminded him. "We gave the evidence we gathered from Ellman's office to Weems. He chose to do nothing about it."

"Right," Nancy chimed in. "Weems was so intent on helping Kreig and Pavin make it look as if the environmentalists were responsible for the bombings, he lost sight of his real job—the security of the facilities and people at the Sports Park."

"He'll pay for it, too," Frank said solemnly. "The police are charging him, along with Kreig and Pavin, for a whole slew of crimes."

Nancy bit into one of the brownies. It was moist and chewy.

"Urich says the state's attorney is really throwing the book at Pavin," she said between chews. "As a senator, he's supposed to represent the people, not swindle them. They've got him on six counts of fraud already. And I bet a search of Pavin's office and records will turn up more."

Joe unsnapped the clamps that bound his boots to the cross-country skis, then went over to sit beside Shana. "How's Tyler doing?" he asked. "I haven't seen him since we rescued him."

Nancy glanced over at Kip's Jeep, which was parked on an old logging road. "They were hoping to get here for lunch. Poor Tyler's been either sleeping, eating, or answering questions for the police. He's going to be one of their main witnesses."

A honk announced the arrival of Allison and Tyler. Nancy waved when they got out of the car. Tyler and Allison strode toward them through the snow, holding hands. Tyler's face was still gaunt, but his long hair was clean and pulled back in a ponytail, and he wore a huge grin.

"We were just talking about you," Nancy said.

"And we were just talking about you guys!" Allison replied. "A herd of reporters pounced on us when we left the police station. We told them Kreig and his thugs would never have been caught if it hadn't been for Nancy Drew and Joe and Frank Hardy."

"I'll drink a toast to that!" Shana said, raising her cup of hot chocolate. "Especially since their quick thinking saved me."

"We're such heroes," Joe joked. He turned to Tyler. "So, Conklin, fill us in on what happened when Kreig and his crew kidnapped you."

"First something to eat." Tyler sat down on a boulder, Allison beside him. "I only had three meals the whole time I was trapped in that gloomy mine." He shuddered. "I doubt if I'll ever be able to go into a dark place like that again."

"I can understand that." Nancy passed them paper plates and sandwiches. As Tyler dug into the food, he told them what happened.

"When I was assigned to city hall, I figured it was the perfect place to gather information to prove Pavin was definitely not pro-environment," he explained. "I started accessing his computer files—uh, not quite legal, of course—and printing out anything that looked interesting."

"Did you know how important that printout of the bankwire receipts was to him?" Nancy asked.

"Not at first. Though it was in a hidden file. I knew because when I went back to that file the next day, someone had erased it. I got a little suspicious. Then Pavin's aides started questioning city hall employees about accessing computer files. That's when I got nervous."

Joe stuffed a third brownie in his mouth. "How'd they track the leak to you?"

"The city employee I was assigned to must have mentioned me. Pavin's aide, Goodwin something, met me on campus one day. He said he'd overlook my breaking into their files if I handed everything over to him."

"That's when Tyler made his mistake," Allison chimed in. "Trying to be the big hero."

Tyler grinned sheepishly. "I told Goodwin to go jump in a lake. That I was going to use whatever I had found to bring Pavin down."

"That was gutsy," Frank commented.

"But stupid, I know," Tyler added. "I had no idea Pavin was such a ruthless sleazeball. I thought he was just greedy."

Allison leaned forward, the glow back in her brown eyes. Nancy was glad to see her friend so happy again. "That night Pavin's goons jumped Tyler on his way home from my dorm."

"And the rest you pretty much know." Tyler smiled gratefully. "I can't thank you guys enough."

"Thank Allison," Nancy insisted. "She never stopped believing in you, even after Kreig and Pavin had set it up to make you look totally guilty."

"They even had Robyn convinced you were a wild radical," Allison told him.

Tyler frowned. "I heard the police confiscated that printing press in the warehouse. Urich was trying to get me to admit I knew about it. But EAAC set it up after I left. I knew the organization was getting more radical. I'm glad I got out in time."

"Now that Pavin's out, maybe Utah can vote in a pro-environment senator," Frank suggested.

Tyler nodded. "Believe me, Peace on Earth will be looking for a good candidate to back."

"So everything turned out okay," Joe said. "We even got the perfect last vacation day."

Just then Kip and George flew past on the snowboards.

"You're leaving tomorrow," Shana said, her mouth drooping.

Joe squeezed her fingers. "Yeah. But just wait. We'll be back for the Utah Winter Games. I wouldn't miss them for anything."

"How about you, Nancy?" Shana asked. "Will you come? They'll be awesome."

"Sounds great."

Allison groaned.

"What's wrong?" Nancy asked. "Did George and I hog all the hot water?"

"No, you guys were great roommates. It's just that if you come out to Salt Lake City again, you have to promise there will be no more kidnappings, chases, or mad bombers. I've had enough excitement for a lifetime!"

Everybody laughed.

"There's no way we can promise that, Allison," Nancy said.

Frank nodded in agreement. "Nancy's right." He draped an arm around her shoulders. "Because whenever the Hardys and Nancy Drew get together, there's bound to be a mystery."

Nancy Drew on Campus™

- ☐ 1 New Lives, New Loves — 52737-1/$3.99
- ☐ 2 On Her Own — 52741-X/$3.99
- ☐ 3 Don't Look Back — 52744-4/$3.99
- ☐ 4 Tell Me The Truth — 52745-2/$3.99
- ☐ 5 Secret Rules — 52746-0/$3.99
- ☐ 6 It's Your Move — 52748-7/$3.99
- ☐ 7 False Friends — 52751-7/$3.99
- ☐ 8 Getting Closer — 52754-1/$3.99
- ☐ 9 Broken Promises — 52757-6/$3.99
- ☐ 10 Party Weekend — 52758-4/$3.99
- ☐ 11 In the Name of Love — 52759-2/$3.99
- ☐ 12 Just the Two of Us — 52764-9/$3.99
- ☐ 13 Campus Exposures — 56802-7/$3.99
- ☐ 14 Hard to Get — 56803-5/$3.99
- ☐ 15 Loving and Losing — 56804-3/$3.99
- ☐ 16 Going Home — 56805-1/$3.99
- ☐ 17 New Beginnings — 56806-X/$3.99
- ☐ 18 Keeping Secrets — 56807-8/$3.99
- ☐ 19 Love On-Line — 00211-2/$3.99
- ☐ 20 Jealous Feelings — 00212-0/$3.99
- ☐ 21 Love and Betrayal — 00213-9/$3.99
- ☐ 22 In and Out of Love — 00214-7/$3.99
- ☐ 23 Otherwise Engaged — 00215-5/$3.99

By Carolyn Keene

Available from Archway Paperbacks